"Hey, Everson!"
Joe called out
in his loudest voice.

The big teenager stopped and turned, still holding the basketball.

"Let me tell you something!" Joe shouted, his voice sounding angry and hurt. "You're not just a menace on the basketball court! You're a menace to the town of Oakdale! For the last time, I want my ball back!"

Wishbone threw out his most ferocious bark in support.

Even from this distance, Wishbone's sharp eyes could see the expression of rage cross Everson's face. Wishbone feared that the teenager was about to run over and do him and Joe some serious physical damage.

The Adventures of WISHBONE™

MOBY DOG

by Alexander Steele

Inspired by *Moby Dick*
by Herman Melville

WISHBONE™ created by Rick Duffield

SCHOLASTIC INC.

New York Toronto London Auckland Sydney
Mexico City New Delhi Hong Kong

ISBN 0-590-03644-0

Copyright © 1998 by Big Feats! Entertainment.
All rights reserved.
Published by Scholastic Inc., 555 Broadway, New York, NY 10012, by arrangement with Lyrick Publishing™.
SCHOLASTIC and associated logos are trademarks and/or registered trademarks of Scholastic Inc.

12 11 10 9 8 7 6 5 4 3 2 1   9/9 0 1 2 3 4/0

Printed in the U.S.A.   40

First Scholastic printing, February 1999

WISHBONE and the **Wishbone** portrait are trademarks and service marks of Big Feats! Entertainment.

Edited by Pam Pollack
Copy edited by Jonathon Brodman
Cover design by Lyle Miller
Interior illustrations by Jane McCreary
Wishbone photograph by Carol Kaelson

To Herman,

who sailed so far in front

he was alone

FROM THE BIG RED CHAIR . . .

Oh . . . hi! Wishbone here. You caught me right in the middle of some of my favorite things—books. Let me welcome you to THE ADVENTURES OF WISHBONE. In each of these books, I have adventures with my friends in Oakdale and imagine myself as a character in one of the greatest stories of all time. This story takes place in the spring, when Joe is twelve and he and his friends are in the sixth grade—during the first season of my television show. In *MOBY DOG,* I imagine I'm Ishmael, a young American sailor from Herman Melville's great novel *MOBY DICK.* It is a story about a seaman's trip on a whaling ship and the chase of a lifetime—the hunt for the mighty Moby Dick!

You're in for a real treat, so pull up a chair and a snack and enjoy *MOBY DOG!*

Chapter One

Wishbone bounded over the squishy, wet ground with enthusiasm. He was eager for action. Rain had drizzled down steadily the past three days, but a few hours ago the sun had finally broken through the clouds. Now Wishbone wanted to take full advantage of the welcome fair weather.

That spring rainy season kept me cooped up forever, the white-with-brown-spots Jack Russell terrier thought. *I need to celebrate my freedom with something really special. Adventure, enlightenment, a sirloin steak—something!*

Wishbone was moving through the densely wooded area near his house. He considered checking out the various tree trunks, but then told himself, "Nah. Been there, done that."

He caught a blur of motion and saw it was a familiar cat slinking by in the distance.

He thought about giving chase, but then said, "Nope, not enough challenge. I can catch that feline with two paws tied behind my back."

Soon Wishbone arrived at his neighbor Wanda Gilmore's front yard, which was next door to his own house.

He was about to dig up one of the many bones he kept buried in the vicinity, but then declared, "No, sir. Dog cannot live on bone alone. There must be something grander awaiting me today!"

K'bam, came a sound from nearby. Wishbone looked up to see a worn orange basketball bounce off a backboard and sink through the net. Joe was playing a little Saturday afternoon basketball with Samantha Kepler, David Barnes, and Damont Jones in the driveway of the house where both Wishbone and Joe lived.

"Beautiful shot," Sam called.

"Thanks," Joe said with an easy smile.

"That shot had your signature all over it," David said as he retrieved the ball. Actually, the ball itself had Joe's signature on it, too. Or at least the first letter of it. A big black "J" had been drawn with a marker on the ball's round surface.

Wishbone trotted over, calling out, "Hey, there, everybody. Nice to see ya. How's it going, Joe?"

Joe Talbot was a good-natured twelve-year-old boy. He had straight brown hair, an athletic body, and a great smile Wishbone always liked to see. Wishbone considered Joe his very best friend in the world. Sometimes he helped Joe out; sometimes Joe helped him. Sometimes Joe fed him dog biscuits; sometimes . . . well, so maybe he never fed Joe anything.

Wishbone sat in the damp grass to watch the game. David took the ball to the end of the driveway, then dribbled in bounds. He had curly black hair and curious eyes. His dribbling was slightly awkward, but Wishbone knew sports weren't as important to David as his many technical projects.

"Come on, throw it over here," Damont called impatiently. The kids were not playing a formal game.

They would pair off into teams for a few points, and then they would switch teams. It was supposed to be fun, but Damont took things a little too seriously. Wishbone could see that the teams at the moment were Damont and David against Sam and Joe.

"Hey, give the kid a chance," Wishbone told Damont. "He just got the ball!"

David stopped as Sam moved up to guard him. She had silky blond hair, pulled back at the moment into a ponytail. There was no one more willing than Sam to lend a hand in time of need. Wishbone and Joe considered Sam and David to be their first-string friends.

"Hey, David," Wishbone advised from his front-row seat. "You know, if I were you, I might try an action-fake to the left, a quick spin to the right, then a fast-break downcourt, ending with a perfectly arched hook shot for the score."

David stood there, still figuring out his move.

Wishbone sighed. All too often, people seemed to ignore his advice. "Fine, don't listen to me."

"Come on, Barnes!" Damont yelled. "Pass the ball!"

Dark-haired Damont was a "sort of" friend of Joe's. He thought he was the best basketball player of the group, and he let everyone know it. Wishbone always kept a close watch on Damont because the boy had a natural talent for causing trouble.

David passed the ball to Damont, who immediately charged like a bull up the driveway. Wishbone could see that he was headed for one of his famous layups. The problem was, Joe ran in front of Damont just before he could leap upward. Damont stood under the basket, wriggling around to look for a shot. But Joe waved his arms, blocking every chance to shoot.

From a short distance back, David called, "Hey, pass it back to me now!"

Wishbone knew Damont didn't want to pass the ball. He wanted to score, all by himself.

"Forget it," Joe teased Damont. "I've got you covered all the way."

Damont blew out a breath of frustration. He did not like being bested by anyone. "Okay, Barnes," he yelled, "here it comes!" Damont heaved the ball in David's direction with all his strength.

The ball flew high over David's head and landed smack in the middle of the street. It bounced a few times, then began to roll away.

"I'll get it," Joe said, moving to chase the runaway ball.

But then Joe saw it wasn't necessary. A teenage boy had appeared on the street. The ball rolled right to him and he stooped to pick it up. Wishbone could see the boy had just stepped out of the wooded area at the end of the block. The woods were a nice place to stroll, and sometimes strangers showed up on the street in this way.

Joe raised his hands to catch the ball. "Thanks," Joe called to the boy. "You can throw it right here."

The teenager looked at Joe. Wishbone had never laid eyes on the kid before. He was a sizable fellow, at least six feet tall and somewhat on the hefty side. Blond hair sloped across his forehead, and his nose lay flat against his face, which reminded Wishbone of a neighborhood bulldog he knew.

"Who's that?" Sam whispered to David.

"I don't know," David whispered back.

The teenager didn't throw the ball. Instead, he tossed it skillfully from one hand to the other, almost looking as if he wanted to join the game. He wore jeans and a dark blue school jacket. On the jacket's front, the words

"Wilson High School" were stitched over an embroidered basketball patch. Wishbone knew Wilson was a high school in a nearby town. The boy's body resembled that of a wrestler, but Wishbone could tell he was an experienced basketballer.

"Hey, come on, big guy," Damont called ut. "Pass it back! We're shooting hoops here!"

Damont had better watch out, Wishbone thought. *That teenager looks as if he could demolish him.*

Still tossing the ball in his hands, the teenage boy shifted his gaze from Joe to Damont.

"What's the matter?" Damont called. "Don't they have enough basketballs at Wilson High School?"

"Damont, cool it," Joe said quietly.

But Damont wasn't done mouthing off. "Maybe not, considering they've lost their last two games!"

The teenager responded with a really angry stare. From where Wishbone stood, he caught a powerful scent of temper coming off the boy.

Without a word, the teenager turned away and began to dribble the ball down the street. Then Wishbone saw the back of the boy's blue jacket. It showed the emblem of a leaping "white whale," which Wishbone figured was the school's mascot.

"Uh . . . excuse me," Joe called after the boy. "You're not taking *my* ball, are you?"

With his back to Joe, the teenager just kept dribbling. It wasn't clear to Wishbone whether the boy was just playing or actually making off with the ball.

Joe turned back to his friends, his face flushed with alarm. "What's he doing?"

"Beats me," David said, looking puzzled.

"Joe, take it easy," Sam said calmly. "I think he might just be having some fun with us."

"No, don't take it easy," Damont told Joe. "You can't just stand there, Talbot. The guy is obviously stealing your ball. Get it back—now!"

Joe looked at Damont, then called out to the teenager. "Hey, whatever-your-name-is, why would you steal a kid's basketball? That's a dumb thing to do!"

Wishbone wasn't used to hearing Joe speak that way. But then Joe wasn't used to having a stranger walk off with his basketball.

The teenager stopped and turned. Now there was something like a taunting look on his face. "If I'm so dumb," he said in a deep voice, "why don't you come and get the ball from me?"

Joe stood there a moment, his eyes glued to the ball. The teenager dribbled the ball under one leg. Wishbone could see Joe tense with anger.

"Joe, don't," Sam said in a low voice. "It's not worth it."

"Go on," Damont whispered.

Joe walked toward the teenager. The teenager dribbled the ball under his other leg. Joe broke into a jog. As Joe approached the boy, Wishbone thought he saw a glint in the teenager's eyes.

Suddenly the teenager spun around and streaked down the street, maneuvering the ball like a professional. Joe turned on the juice and ran after him.

"Oh, no!" Wishbone called, his four legs flying after Joe. "You're not doing this without me, pal. That guy's a lot bigger than you are. Come to think of it, he's a lot bigger than me, too, but I've got a black belt in defensive action."

At top speed, the teenager reached the end of the block and turned right. Joe and Wishbone followed in hot pursuit. "Hey, please come back here!" Joe called to the boy. "I really need that ball back!"

As Wishbone ran, he kept his eyes focused on the "white whale" emblem that appeared to be leaping across the back of the teenager's jacket.

Just as Joe and Wishbone gained some ground, the teenager expertly palmed the basketball and darted through a nearby yard. Wishbone thought they might catch him now because the boy was headed straight for a wooden fence. Except—using one hand, the teenager grabbed the fence's cross-beam and pulled himself upward, keeping hold of the basketball with his other hand. Wishbone saw the "white whale" emblem disappear over the top of the fence.

Moments later, Wishbone watched as Joe grabbed onto the fence's cross-beam and pulled himself up. Joe didn't climb over, though. Instead, he slapped a frustrated hand against the fence and muttered, "Ah, it's no use. He's already over the fence on the other side."

Joe dropped to the ground, breathing hard.

"I'm sorry," Wishbone said between his panting. "I should have snagged his trousers before he hit the fence."

"I really hate to lose that ball," Joe said, kicking the curb in frustration.

Wishbone looked up at his best friend with great sympathy. "I'm really sorry," he said. "Honest to dog, I did my best."

Joe stood there a moment, then began to head back toward his house. "Well, I guess it's gone now," he said to himself. "Unless I can figure out a way to get it back."

You know, something smells very familiar here— the part about pursuing a white whale, I mean. I'm reminded of one of the biggest adventure stories of all time. A tale that's totally awesome in both size and scope. An epic drama that is just begging me to enter its pages.

It's a book about whaling, and it was written in the year 1851 by Herman Melville. The book's author knew all about whaling. As a young man, he dared to go out to sea on several whaling trips himself, and some of the elements in his book were inspired by real-life events.

I tell you, the mere mention of this book's title makes my heart swell and pound and roll with excitement. If you haven't guessed it by now, I'm referring to the great novel *Moby Dick!*

Chapter Two

Wishbone drifted deep into his imagination. He pictured himself as a restless young American man in the middle of the 1800s. That fellow's name was Ishmael, and he told the story of *Moby Dick*.

Call me Ishmael. Why? Because that's my name.

Some time ago, I decided to sail around a bit and see the watery part of the world. You see, whenever I get that damp and drizzly feeling in my soul, whenever I start growling and snapping at everyone who passes by, I know it's time to leave the land for a while.

I never sail as an average passenger, though. Traveling in this manner is costly and, besides, passengers just lay about getting seasick a lot. No, when I go to sea, I go as a simple sailor. True, the grub's not always great, and you have to work your tail off, and those captains tend to be awfully bossy. But the sailor's life is the only way to fully experience the high adventure and deep thought that the ocean offers a man.

Having four strong legs, I had managed to get myself a job on several merchant ships in the past. However, these were just brief trips hauling cargo from one port to another. This time I vowed to sail on the longest and most daring type of sea quest imaginable—a voyage on a whaling vessel!

Ever been whaling, mates? In those days, whaling was a really big deal. This was because people didn't have electricity back then, so all the lighting came from oil lamps, lanterns, and candles. And most of these were fueled with whale oil. Of course, in order to get the oil, you first had to catch a whale. And did I mention that whales are the largest creatures that ever lived?

Aye, so I packed a bag, took it between my teeth, and journeyed to the whaling village of New Bedford, Massachusetts. The night was bitingly cold, and I wasted no time in entering what appeared to be the town's least expensive inn—the Spouter Inn, to be precise.

I moved through a dimly lit room, past a table of rough seamen who filled the air with tobacco smoke and noisy laughter. My little black nose is especially sensitive, and, let me say, the men didn't smell very sweet. Finally, I found the landlord, a crusty old man with the frightening name of Peter Coffin. When I told the fellow I'd like a room for the next two nights, he said, "Got no vacant rooms. You'll have to share a bed with a harpooner."

I didn't relish the idea of sharing a bed with any stranger, let alone a harpooner. But the hour was late and my fur was thoroughly chilled. "Very well, I'll take it," I told Coffin. "Tell me, is this harpooner one of the men at this table?"

"Nope," Coffin said, wiping a greasy hand on his apron.

"Is he in the room already?"

"Nope."

"Then where in the world is he?" I asked.

"He's out peddling."

"Peddling what?"

"He's out peddling heads," Coffin replied with a grim grin.

I figured the man was joshing me. So I had a quick supper of leftovers, lapped up some water, then went upstairs to my room. It looked clean enough, at least by the dim glow of a candle. Dog-tired by now, I blew out the light, then leaped up on the bed and crawled under a blanket. The bed was terribly uncomfortable, especially knowing that the missing harpooner would soon be lying in it beside me. Nevertheless, I managed to doze.

Sometime later, I heard the door creak open. A figure trudged into the room and placed a candle on a shelf.

Then he set a blackened object on the shelf. As my eyes adjusted, I realized it was a shrunken human head. But that alone wasn't so terrible. On certain South Seas islands, I knew, heads of dead people were shrunken down to miniature size and sold as souvenirs. Suddenly, I understood what Coffin meant by "peddling heads."

By the flickering candle flame, I caught a glimpse of the harpooner himself. He was a very large man. His own head was a bald dome, and his whole face was stained a purplish-yellow color. As the man undressed, I saw that bizarre figures and symbols ran up and down his entire body. I felt my fur bristle. With horror, I realized the man was tattooed from head to foot in the fashion of the South Seas *cannibals*. Yes, the man who was about to enter my bed was not just a harpooner, but an eater of people!

I held my breath and forced my tail to be still. Obviously, the cannibal had not noticed me yet. He blew out the candle.

Just as I was about to flee through the darkness, the cannibal pulled down the blanket and climbed in the bed beside me. His hand touched one of my floppy ears.

The cannibal jerked away and cried shrilly, "Who-ee you?"

I spoke, just barely. "Well, I'm . . . uh . . . Oh, I'm just . . ."

"Speak! Tell me who-ee be, or I kill-ee!"

"No, don't do that! No kill-ee, please!"

"Speak, or I'll kill-ee."

I shouted for the landlord at the top of my lungs. "Peter Coffin! Get in here, man!"

A moment later, the landlord shoved open the door and asked gruffly, "What are you singing about at this hour?"

"You didn't tell me my bedmate was to be a cannibal!" I barked with rage.

"I told you he was selling heads," Coffin replied. "It should have been obvious enough that he was from the cannibal part of the world. Nothing to fear, though. Queequeg, here, is one of the most well behaved cannibals you could ever hope to meet." Then Coffin spoke to the cannibal in a soothing tone. "It's all right, Queequeg. He stay-ee in your bed. It's all right."

Queequeg grunted with apparent understanding, and Coffin left the room. Immediately, Queequeg settled into a sleeping position. Realizing the man wasn't about to eat me, at least not this night, I dropped my head upon the pillow. And, to be honest, I never slept better in my entire life.

I awoke the following morning to find one of the cannibal's arms resting upon the fur of my back. *He's just a wee bit too close for comfort,* I thought. Not wishing to be the fellow's breakfast, I quietly jumped off the bed and left the room.

It was a dreary winter's day, but, after some breakfast and hot coffee, I strolled around the town a bit. America sent out more whaling vessels than any other country, and New Bedford was the most successful of its whaling villages. As a result, the shops, homes, and cobblestoned streets were charmingly picturesque. And, there were plenty of nice trees, too.

As it was Sunday, I went into a chapel. Fittingly, it was decorated with a whale theme. Marble plaques adorned the walls, to represent loved ones lost on whaling trips. And, believe it or not, the pulpit was an exact replica of a ship's wooden bow.

The chapel was packed with people, so I just lay on the floor near the back. While I waited for the service to begin, I did some personal grooming with my tongue. Then I saw an unexpected person enter the place—Queequeg, the cannibal! He took a seat in the pew right next to me. He sat there quite calm, not seeing me or speaking to anyone else. I doubted he was a regular churchgoer. But I suppose, like me, he wanted to see what this chapel had to offer. Noticing that his hand was a shade of nutmeg-brown, I realized that must be his original skin color. The cannibal wore ordinary clothing and, despite the fact he had a purplish-yellow face, he looked surprisingly respectable.

At last, a barrel-chested old man with white hair and a beard climbed a rope ladder to the pulpit. This was a famous chaplain by the name of Father Mapple—he was a former seaman himself.

"Shipmates," Father Mapple called out in a thunderous voice, "today I will deliver a sermon on the biblical tale of Jonah—the man who fled to sea and found himself swallowed alive by the jaws of a Leviathan."

In case you're wondering, "Leviathan" is what a whale is called in the Bible. Somehow I get the feeling

this guy delivers a sermon on Jonah and the whale *every* Sunday.

"But think not this is only an adventurous tale of the sea," Father Mapple continued. "Nay, my friends, there is much more to this story than meets the eye. Indeed, there is much more to most of what we see than meets the eye. I warn you, do not judge anything too quickly. For, I daresay, almost everything in this gigantic universe of ours contains many meanings."

These words made sense to me. I looked over at Queequeg and realized I had perhaps judged *him* too quickly. *After all,* I thought seriously, *just because a man is a cannibal doesn't necessarily mean he's a bad fellow, does it?*

I looked back at the chaplain and listened to the rest of the sermon, which was quite inspiring. By the time Father Mapple bowed his head and prepared for one final prayer, I noticed Queequeg had left.

Returning to my room, I nudged open the door with my muzzle and found Queequeg now going through his own type of prayer. Squatted on the floor, he was staring at a small figurine, which I assumed was a religious idol from his native island. All the while he spoke in a very low voice.

I watched him from the doorway. Despite his wild appearance, I sensed that the savage had a simple, honest heart. There was also a certain nobility to the shape of his head that reminded me in a strange way of George Washington. Then and there, I decided I would offer my friendship to this man, if he would have it.

Soon Queequeg rose from the floor. Next he did a curious thing. After mixing up a lather from soap and water, he rubbed some on his head and face. Then he picked up his whaling harpoon, a spearlike weapon with a sharp triangular barb at the tip. My ears shifted with confusion.

To my surprise, Queequeg began shaving his head with the harpoon's barb as if it were a razor.

"Uh . . . hello there, Queequeg," I said from the doorway.

He turned and said politely, "Hello. Will you be sleep with me again?"

"I believe so," I said, realizing his English was not so bad.

"That is good-ee," he said, as he continued shaving with the harpoon.

I moved cautiously into the room. "Uh . . . tell me something. Do you cannibal fellows eat . . . well, just anyone?"

Queequeg smiled wide, showing teeth that were filed into very sharp daggers. "No, we do not. We eat only enemy from battle. Barbecue them and put parsley in mouth. Taste very good-ee."

My stomach turned a little. I'm very fond of meat and bones myself, but not when they belong to someone I've actually met. I dared to ask, "I'm not your enemy, am I?"

"No. I like you be my friend."

"Ah, well, the feeling is mutual," I said, leaping up on the bed. Then I told Queequeg a little about myself, and he told me a little about himself. Before long, an icy sleet tapped at the windowpane. Not to be frozen, the two of us got a fire dancing in the small fireplace, and that little room of ours became quite cozy. My tail began to swish back and forth with contentment.

Queequeg, it turned out, came from the faraway island of Kokovoko, where his father was the king and his uncle was the high priest. As a young man, Queequeg had boarded a whaling vessel because he wanted to have a good look at the civilized world. However, he didn't much like what he saw, so he learned to use a harpoon and took up the profession of whaling. Like myself, he was now in search of a whaling vessel on which to make a voyage.

I had to laugh. The previous night I had considered this fellow the lowest form of humanity. Lower even than a cat. Now I saw him differently. I realized he was a prince by birth, and a prince in manners, as well.

"Queequeg, I have a plan," I said around the time night darkened the window. "How about you and me going on a whaling voyage together-ee?"

Queequeg ruffled the fur on my neck with enthusiasm and cried out, "Yes! Together-ee!"

Then, as a symbol of our eternal friendship, he made a gift to me of the shrunken head.

Wishbone's Useful Ship Dictionary

So that all ye landlubbers don't get lost at sea, here are some terms that will guide ye as ye make yer way around and about the *Pequod*.

avast!   a direct order to stop doing something, and fast!

aye   a seafarer's way of saying "yes"

bow   the front of the ship

chart a course   to work with seafaring diagrams and instruments (like a compass) to make a "map" of where the ship will sail on its journey. It's like a water version of a road map (also called "plotting a course").

course   a route or path

deck   the open-air floor area of the ship

gangplank   a narrow wooden walkway (sometimes wobbly) leading from the dock area up to the ship.

gunwale   (pronounced *gun'l*) the wooden railing that runs around the ship's deck

helm   all the steering equipment, including the steering wheel itself. It's located on the quarterdeck.

hold   a storage area at the lowest level of the ship

hull   the entire body of the ship

larboard   the ship's left side

mast	the very tall pole from which a sail is hung. From bow to stern, the masts are called: foremast, mainmast, and mizzenmast.
masthead	the very top part of the mast
mate	an officer on a sailing ship who ranks below the captain. The three types of mate are: chief, second, and third. "Mate" is also used as a friendly greeting from one sailor to another.
merchant ship	a ship used for hauling goods and passengers from one port to another the back-and-forth
pitch	rocking and rolling motion of a ship at sea. Most sailors find this soothing; others head for the nearest railing!
quadrant	a brass device used for gauging a ship's direction, based on the sun's position
quarterdeck	a raised portion of the deck toward the stern
rigging	all the many ropes abovedeck. Some are used as ladders, some to control the sails, and some to hold things in place.
starboard	the ship's right side
stern	the back of the ship
stowaway	a person who sneaks aboard ship without paying, or is not a listed crew member. Often he or she is out to get a free ride from one port to another.
typhoon	a tropical storm (similar to a hurricane) that forms mostly in the western Pacific Ocean
wake	a trail, like a frothy white-water path, left behind an object moving through the water. A wake can be made by a ship, or by a large sea creature like a whale.

Chapter Three

When Monday arrived, Queequeg and I sailed on a small ship to a tiny island off the Massachusetts coast. This lonely stretch of sand is Nantucket. True, I could have found a suitable whaling vessel in New Bedford, but for the sake of history, I chose Nantucket. This is where the American whaling industry first grew to its present greatness.

My tattooed friend and I found an inn, where we supped from bowls of chowder, a savory mixture of cream, pork, spices, and the juiciest of clams. Delicious! I licked up every drop, and then some. Again Queequeg and I shared a room for the night and we got along very well.

The following morning, we made our way to the harbor. The wharf was crammed with whaling vessels, which are built wider and sturdier than the average ship. Sails flapped from the tall masts, and riggings of rope extended every which way. Though the day was gloomy, the heavily salted air refreshed my nose and set my tail wagging happily. Queequeg and I spent a few moments gazing at the vast gray ocean that lay before us.

"Big-ee," Queequeg remarked.

"Yes, very big-ee," I agreed. "That's why I like it."

After asking around, I discovered that three whaling vessels were scheduled to sail soon. I spent a good deal of time examining each one. Queequeg left the decision to me, and I ended up choosing the *Pequod*. I'm not sure why. Its wood was by far the most weather-stained, and its three bare masts stood like a trio of stiff, old kings. Perhaps the *Pequod*'s special look of nobility appealed to me, or perhaps it was simply a matter of fate that led me to choose this ship.

As Queequeg wandered down the wharf to look at something, I trotted across the gangplank leading to the *Pequod*. A variety of supplies and equipment lay scattered about the deck. The ship was obviously being prepared for its long journey, but since it was almost noon, there was no one working. I sniffed around a bit, my nails clicking loudly on the ship's wooden surface. Eventually, I spotted a man on the quarterdeck and climbed up to him.

He sat at a table, upon which a stack of papers was weighted down by a piece of whalebone. In addition to the papers, there was a leather-bound book, a quill pen, and an inkwell. He was a chubby, red-cheeked fellow at least seventy years of age. His leathery skin and crow-footed eyes indicated that he was an experienced man of the sea.

"Are you the *Pequod*'s captain?" said I.

The man peered down at me and said, "Supposing I am, lad?"

"I should like to sail with you."

He gave a hearty chuckle. "Dost thou know *anything* of whaling, young fellow?"

"No, sir, but I've made several voyages in the merchant service, and I'm a quick learner."

He slapped a hand on the table. "Flukes! Don't aggravate me with talk of the merchant service! The merchant service is like a romp in the park compared to whaling! Tell me, art thou willing to spend three long years—that's how long it'll be—without taking a single step on land? And, tell me, art thou willing to risk life and limb racing after a whale a hundred times thy size in nothing but a flimsy rowboat?"

I lifted my ears and flexed the muscles in all four of my legs. I was doing my best to appear strong and brave. "Sir, I have determined to go a'whaling. Whatever task is required, I'll do it—and do it tip-top well."

"Why, you're a spirited lad, aren't ye?" the man said, his face wrinkling into a smile. "All righty, then, maybe a'whaling you'll go. My name's Peleg. No, I'm not the captain. That'll be Ahab. Me and my partner, Bildad, we own this proud ol' ship." Then he bellowed out, "Bildad!"

Soon Bildad appeared. He was a sea veteran of Peleg's age, but rather serious and thin.

"This young man says he wants to go to sea on the *Pequod*," Peleg told Bildad.

"Dost thee?" Bildad said in a suspicious tone.

Again I tried to look strong and brave. "I dost."

Bildad eyed me from head to tail, then said flatly, "He'll do."

Immediately, Peleg flung open the leather-bound volume. "There, see, my adventure-seeking mate, ye got your wish. Tell me, Bildad, what lay shall we give this fine young fellow?"

Let me explain. You see, no one on a whaling vessel was paid a regular wage. Food and shelter were free, of course. After that, every crew member received a share of the profits from the precious whale oil gathered on the voyage. These shares were termed "lays," and the size of a crew member's lay depended upon his importance to the ship.

"He shall have the seven hundred and seventy-seventh lay," Bildad murmured. I knew this was a small one.

Peleg sprang up and slapped his partner roughly on the shoulder. "Why, blast your eyes, Bildad, the lad must have more than that! I'm putting him down for the three-hundredth lay."

Peleg returned to his chair and scribbled something in the big book. Then he set the book and inkwell down on the deck.

The lay Peleg offered me was still smaller than I had expected, but it was good enough. I stuck one of my front paws in the ink and signed the book.

As Peleg picked up the book and inkwell, Queequeg finally walked over. "Ah, yes, this is my good friend, Queequeg," said I. "He also wants to sail on the *Pequod*. He's a harpooner. Killed more whales than I can count."

Peleg and Bildad studied my friend's purplish-yellow face. "A heathen—he does not believe in our Lord," Bildad said with distaste.

"Aye, maybe not," Peleg argued, "but what god he worships ain't half so important as how well he can heave his harpoon into a sperm whale's hump!"

Queequeg had actually brought his harpoon along, and now I realized why. He gestured at a wooden crate that lay some distance across the deck. "Look-ee at that box," he said. "Look-ee at speck of tar on side."

Queequeg lifted the long weapon and sent it flying through the air. *K'thunk*—the harpoon stuck in the crate right next to the speck of tar.

"Why, flukes and flames!" Peleg cried out with delight. "We must have this savage aboard! Amazing aim! Hedgehog . . . Quohog . . . whatever your name is, we must have ye! I'm putting ye down for the ninetieth lay! Higher than I ever paid a harpooner!"

Peleg's excitement was understandable, considering that harpooners were among the most important members of the crew.

"You should see him shave with that thing," I joked.

Peleg quickly scribbled in the book, then handed Queequeg the pen. With pride, Queequeg drew a little symbol in place of his name. Bildad scoffed, then walked away, muttering something about "not trusting heathens the least bit."

"We'll be shipping at dawn two days from now," Peleg informed me and Queequeg. "Christmas Day, in fact. Come ready for the grandest ride of your life! And three years from that day, I'll have a hot supper smoking for ye in old Nantucket!"

"It's a deal," I said, licking my chops and wagging my tail. "But . . . uh . . . well . . . before I go, I would like to see the captain."

A cloud seemed to pass over Peleg's face. "What for?"

"I shall be under this man's command for a very long time. It's only natural I should want to meet him."

"I'm afraid that won't be possible," Peleg said with some discomfort. "Ahab's keeping in his house these days. Ever since the last . . . Well, you see, he's sort of sick . . . no, he ain't sick, exactly, but . . . he ain't well, either. Fear not, he's a good man. Not merry, but . . . I tell thee, it's better to sail with a moody, good captain than a laughing, bad one."

"I see," I said, not really understanding at all.

Our business done, Queequeg and I left the *Pequod* and walked along the wharf. Almost at once, a shabbily dressed man who gave off a strong odor of fish came up to us. He hurled a pointed finger at us and asked, "Have ye signed on for the *Pequod,* mates?"

"Why, yes," said I. "Just now. Who are you?"

"The name's Elijah." The man spoke rather fast. "Just like the biblical prophet. And I'm wondering if that book you signed mentioned anything about giving up your soul. And I wonder if they told ye much about your captain. Ahab's his name. Just like one of the Bible's most awful villains."

So that you know, in those days it was common for Americans to have biblical names. In fact, the name "Ishmael" also comes from the Bible—where he was a boy given away by his family.

"They told me Ahab is a good captain," I replied, irritated by the man. Calm as ever, Queequeg watched a seagull soar over the water.

Elijah knelt down to me, a strange look in his eye. "Then I suppose they didn't tell ye nothing about what happened to Ahab on his last voyage—how one of his legs was chewed up and crunched by the biggest monster of a whale that ever attacked a boat. How the pain from his bloody stump shot into his brain like lightning bolts. How he's never been right in the mind since. I suppose they didn't tell ye any of that, did they? Well, I'm telling ye these things now as a sort of warning to ye. But then . . . what's signed is signed. What's to be, will be. Ain't that right?"

"Look here," I said firmly. "Mr. Peleg and Mr. Bildad are wise to the ways of the sea. And I'm sure they would not entrust their valuable ship to a captain who did not deserve the responsibility."

Elijah gave out a raspy laugh. "Is that what ye think, is it? Ah, well, I'm sorry I stopped ye. 'Morning to ye, shipmates!"

The ragged man scurried down the wharf. I paused a moment, then glanced back at the towering masts of the *Pequod*. My whiskers gave a slight twitch. I confess, I was beginning to feel a ripple of nervousness about this unseen captain. After all, the man was to be my complete master for the next three years. But then I told myself to think nothing of it.

Now, before I set off on this whaling expedition, maybe I should take a quick trip back to Oakdale. Captain Ahab may have lost a leg, but let's not forget—my best buddy, Joe, also lost something.

Chapter Four

"I don't see that ball in your hands," Damont called.

"I didn't get it," Joe said, as he and Wishbone returned to the Talbots' front yard. "That guy from Wilson had some real moves."

"Well, let's just get another ball," David said, trying to keep the situation upbeat. "Want me to go get one?"

Joe shook his head. "No, I don't feel like playing anymore."

Sam smiled at Joe. "Come on, it's only a ball. You've got several others."

Joe's face suddenly became very serious. Wishbone knew something else was going on, and from the look on Sam's face, she knew it, too.

Finally, Joe said, "My dad gave me that ball just before he died."

Wishbone felt his heart sink. He had forgotten Joe's dad had given him that ball. But now he remembered that Mr. Talbot had given Joe the ball just a few weeks before he had died of a rare blood disorder. Wishbone nuzzled himself against Joe's leg.

Sam immediately stepped forward and she gave

Joe a gentle pat on the shoulder. "I'm really sorry, Joe. I didn't realize that."

"Why don't we sit down and figure this thing out," David advised. At that, everyone headed for the Talbots' front porch. Joe and Sam took seats on the hanging swing-chair, while David sat on the deck. Damont lingered at the deck's railing, a little distance apart from the others.

Wishbone lay faithfully at Joe's feet, as he always did when things got tough. For a few moments there was no sound but the steady creak of the swing. Then Joe said with annoyance, "Why did that Wilson kid steal my ball?"

"Hard to say," David replied. "Maybe the guy just goes around stealing stuff. Or maybe something you or Damont said just pushed the wrong button. Or . . . oh, I don't know, there could be a lot of explanations."

Joe stared straight ahead. "I wonder if there's a way to get the ball back."

Wishbone knew Joe could be a very determined boy. He would struggle tirelessly with a complex math problem or spend hours perfecting his jump shot. But he was also very reasonable, not the type who would go looking for trouble.

"I'm sure there's a way to get the ball back," Sam said. "A diplomatic way that won't get this Wilson kid all riled up. We just need to put our heads together and figure out what to do."

"True," Wishbone said. "Sam is making a very good point here."

"I remember the day my dad gave me that ball," Joe said, pretending to grip it in his hands. "First he put my initial on it. Then we went outside and started shooting baskets. He was coaching me, and after what seemed like forever, I finally sank a shot. I guess that was the start of my basketball career."

Wishbone looked up at Joe. "I remember how proud I was of you that day. I was just a puppy then. An awfully cute little fellow, as I recall."

Damont had been listening to this whole conversation from the porch railing. Then he walked slowly over to Sam and said, "Could I sit there a sec?"

Sam got up, reluctantly, and Damont sat on the swing-chair next to Joe. Damont placed an arm around Joe's shoulder. "Joe, next year you and I are probably going to be playing together on the school team, right?"

"That's right," Joe said.

"And I'm your buddy, right?"

"Sure, I guess so."

"And you trust me, right?"

Joe hesitated. "I don't know if I'd go that far, but what's on your mind?"

"This guy robbed you," Damont said, showing a clenched fist. "He swiped that ball right out from under your nose. And there's only one explanation why he would do that."

"What is it?" Joe asked.

"He meant it as a personal insult. He took one look at you and thought to himself, 'I'm better than this little squirt, and I'm going to prove it to him.' Believe me, I know the type."

I bet you do, Wishbone thought.

"Why would that Wilson kid want to prove anything to me?" Joe asked. "It doesn't make sense. I've never even seen him before."

"Because he's mean," Damont stated flatly. "He's just plain mean."

"Well, yeah, maybe he is," Joe said thoughtfully.

A cloud passed over the sun, darkening the yard.

"Don't you see?" Damont kept on. "Us nice people of the world have to take a stand against the mean people. We've got to show them they can't push us around. What I'm saying is, it's your duty to go after that big oaf and demand your ball back!"

"I hate to say it," Wishbone commented, "but I think Damont, here, may have a point. Bullies have to be stopped."

"Maybe you're right," Joe said with a slight nod.

"'Cause let me tell you something," Damont continued. "Laid-back tactics aren't going to work with a guy like that. In this type of situation, you've got to go all the way. Throw caution to the wind. And you can't stall, either. By sundown, who knows where that ball might be?"

"That's true," Joe said quietly.

"I know you'll do the right thing," Damont told Joe. "And I'll tell you what. If you need some muscle, just give me a call."

"Give you a call?" Joe said. "Where are you going?"

Damont swung up to his feet. "I've got some stuff to take care of around town. If you need me, leave a message with my mom. She usually knows where to find me. Later, everyone." Damont gave Joe a rough pat on the shoulder, then left the porch and tramped through the yard.

"He's doing it again," Sam said, returning to the swing-chair. "Damont starts stirring things up, and then he leaves."

"But in this case, Damont may be right," Joe said, watching his sort-of friend swagger down the street. "I really should try to get hold of that guy."

"Come on," David said, kneeling beside Joe. "You know better than to listen to Damont about anything."

"Joe, you'd be crazy to tangle with that high-school boy," Sam argued. "Compared to you, he's a giant."

36

Wishbone was watching the conversation as if it were a tennis match.

"I didn't say I was going to tangle with him," Joe said. "I just need to catch up with him and get my ball back."

Hmm, Wishbone thought. *This is an interesting problem. On the one paw, I agree with Sam and David, but on the other paw, I agree with Joe.*

"Maybe there's a way to find out who this guy is," Sam offered. "Then we'd be able to get in touch with him when we've decided what sort of approach to use."

"Good idea," David said eagerly. "It shouldn't be that difficult finding out his name. From his jacket, we know he goes to Wilson High School and we know he plays on the basketball team. Hey, we could probably track him down on the Internet!"

Joe ran a hand through his hair, thinking matters through. "Okay," he said. "It's a start, at least. Yeah, the Internet's not a bad idea. Come on, crew, let's do it!"

Joe sprang to his feet with renewed hope. Then Wishbone led the gang across the yard toward David's house, which was just next door.

All right, while we're setting off to sail the seas of the Internet, it's time for Ishmael to sail off on the real seas. Hope you're not the type who gets seasick easily. Anchors aweigh!

Chapter Five

As Christmas Day dawned gray and misty, Queequeg and I carried our few possessions toward the *Pequod*. I no longer held any doubts about the captain, but just before my friend and I boarded the ship, something very bizarre happened.

I glimpsed five shadowy shapes moving silently and swiftly down the gangplank. In the eerie twilight, they seemed almost ghostly. Queequeg and I crossed the gangplank shortly after them, but by the time I stepped on deck, the shapes had vanished. My trusty black nose couldn't even pick up their scents.

"That's awfully odd," I told Queequeg, still sniffing around for the missing men. "They seem to have disappeared."

Nothing made Queequeg nervous. He shrugged and said, "Many things odd I see in America."

After storing my possessions, I climbed to the quarterdeck for my last look at land for a long time to come. A seagull swooped over the wharf, screaming out a farewell to me. I saw the ship's owners, Peleg and Bildad, leaving the ship for the final time. There was still no sign of

Captain Ahab about. I knew, however, that captains sometimes left the departure from the harbor in the hands of the officers, while they were busy charting courses in their cabin.

"Heave the anchor!" a voice rang out. The anchor cranked noisily upward, three ivory sails swelled from the masts, and the *Pequod* plunged into the wide Atlantic Ocean.

I jumped down to the main deck and raced past the masts and rigging, finally stopping at the ship's bow. Rising on my hind legs, I put my front paws up on the gunwale, the railing that ran around the deck. My heart leaped with excitement. The gray waves of the Atlantic Ocean rolled outward, seemingly all the way to infinity. I took a deep breath of sea air and felt the freezing spray on my fur. *Ah, let other young men have their college education,* I thought. *This voyage shall be both Harvard and Yale to me.*

"No time for gawking, ye ragamuffins!" a voice hollered. We were put to work right away, organizing equipment and adjusting the sails. This last task we did by pulling on long ropes and sometimes climbing up the masts on roped ladders.

I also began to meet my fellow sailors, of which there were about two dozen. Though this was an American ship, most of the crew came from far-off corners of the globe. Most wore crude britches and short coats known as "monkey jackets," and every man's skin was sun-toughened into what looked like leather. They were a rugged group. In fact, while on land, you'd cross the street to avoid many of them.

At one point Queequeg approached with two men who were as hulking and muscular as himself. "This be my friend, Ishmael," Queequeg said, making introductions all around. "Ishmael, these be other two harpooners. Tashtego and Dagoo."

"Hallo," Tashtego said, almost crushing my paw with a handshake. He was a North American Indian with red-tinted skin and long black hair. This man's ancestors had been the very first American whale hunters.

"Greeting," Dagoo said, almost breaking my neck with a friendly rub. He was an African with coal-black skin and two earrings of hooped gold. He had merely traded in the tiger-and-lion hunt of his native land for whale hunting.

"It's a pleasure to meet you both," I told the men. I meant it, too. A few days ago, I might have been wary of these two fellows so different from myself. But my friendship with Queequeg had taught me a valuable lesson. A man can be honest in any sort of skin . . . or fur, for that matter.

We worked until sunset streaked the sky with splendid shades of purple and red. Then came one of our most important duties—eating supper.

First supper was served to the captain and his officers in a cabin beneath the quarterdeck. Then the harpooners, carpenter, and blacksmith were served in the same cabin. Last but not least, the crew was served. Since the crew didn't have a dining cabin, we usually took our meals on the open deck, which was fine by me.

Oh, we never got anything so delightful as creamy clam chowder, but, with a cook and serving-boy aboard, we never lacked for chow. While gobbling up my food by the foremast, I had a pleasant conversation with sailors from Denmark, France, and China.

Just as I licked the last morsel off my platter, the three officers approached. The captain, of course, was top dog, but directly under him were these three men. Though each of them came from Massachusetts, it was funny how different they were in personality.

"Fellows, how's the grub?" asked the chief mate, Starbuck. He was a handsome man with an air of responsibility about him. Since Captain Ahab had not yet appeared, Starbuck was temporarily in charge of the crew.

"Not so delicious as pastries and crêpes," a Frenchman said with a chuckle.

"Or roasted duck with noodles," a Chinese man said with a bow of his head.

"Or a bone still greasy with meat," I added.

Stubb, the second mate, spoke. "Soon as I can, lads, I'll change the nightly menu to whale steak. It'll be plenty tender compared to that shoe leather the cook passes off as beef." Stubb was a jolly fellow who found most everything in life to be a great joke.

Flask, the third mate, spoke. "The cook's food is just fine for me, thank you." He was a simple man who didn't seem to spend much thought on anything.

"Why has the captain not come up?" a Danish man asked, knowing the mates had just suppered with him.

"I'm afraid the captain is slightly ill," Starbuck informed us. "Nothing to fear. Ahab's a hardy man, and he'll be good as new any day now."

As the sky dimmed to blackness, the serving-boy cleared away the platters and mugs. I lay down, feeling the cool wooden deck beneath my belly. My sense of hearing is very sharp, and I listened as the old ship groaned and creaked with every roll of the sea. The officers carried on a conversation with the carpenter and blacksmith up on the quarterdeck. Queequeg possessed a very long pipe, and he shared a smoke by the bow with the two other harpooners, Tashtego and Dagoo. Several more men wandered over to relax with me and my companions at the foremast.

"Where are you from?" I asked a grizzled man, who was by far the eldest among us.

"The Isle of Man," the man replied. "A rocky isle off the coast of England. They call the likes of me a Manxman."

"I've never met a Manxman before," said I. "Truth is, I've never been whaling, either."

"Aye, well, this whaling is a noble profession," the Manxman said with pride. "Some fellows make fun of our trade, call it a butchering business. But, upon my soul, most every lamp and candle round the globe burns as a shrine to our glory."

A man from Australia stretched his arms and spoke. "And you know, the whaling ships were the first to discover many parts of the world. Why, nobody paid much attention to great big ol' Australia till the whalers told them about it."

A man from Portugal raised a finger. "And, let us not forget—at the crowning ceremony of a brand-new king or queen, the head is anointed with what? The sweet oil of a sperm whale!"

We had a good laugh at this remark. That led to a series of colorful jokes being told. Attracted to the laughter, three other men wandered over—an American, a Dutchman, and a Brazilian.

Soon the air grew colder and a million stars glittered above like crystals of ice. We warmed ourselves with more merriment. A man from Sicily brought out a tambourine, which he jangled gently as we sang an old sea song. I howled along with the best of them:

> *"Farewell and adieu to you, Spanish ladies.*
> *Farewell and adieu to you, ladies of Spain.*
> *For we've received orders for to sail for Old England,*
> *And we hope in a short time to see you again."*

"And I've met many a Spanish lady!" called a man who steered the big wooden wheel at the helm. Of course he had. The man was from Spain!

Then the tambourine beat became livelier as we engaged in a variety of dances. When it comes to dancing, I'm the owner of four left feet, but I tell you, some of those tough sailors kicked up a leg pretty good. Things became truly comical when a man from Tahiti taught an island dance called the "Heeva Heeva" to a man from Iceland.

"The world's nothing but a gigantic ball," the Manx-man said cheerfully. "So I say it's right to make the whole world a ballroom. And that includes the deck of this humble ship!"

Ah, yes, it was a wonderful time. That night I could feel the crew begin to form into a closely knit pack. I also felt I had made a friend from almost every portion of the Earth.

Finally, it was time for another very important duty, sleeping. The crew slept in bunks that were crowded together in a damp chamber belowdecks. Nothing about the room was comfortable, and when the water roughened, you had to be careful you didn't go flying from bunk to floor. But I was tired enough to get a deeply peaceful sleep.

Indeed, I slept well every night—at least for the first week. After that, I found myself awakened every midnight by a strange clomping noise.

thum-Clunk . . . thum-Clunk . . . thum-Clunk . . .

The sound came from up above on the deck, which was only several feet over my head. It would have bothered me even if my hearing wasn't so sharp. I also noticed that the sound made several other sailors toss and turn.

One day I asked Queequeg about the odd nightly sound. He wasn't aware of it, though, and I kept myself from questioning anyone else. I thought the answer might be so obvious as to make me appear foolish. I was a little bit sensitive to this sort of thing, seeing how I was new to the whaling game, and a bit smaller than the rest of the crew.

After about ten days, however, I discovered the source of the sound. One brisk morning as I went about the deck sweeping, I finally saw him—Captain Ahab.

Making his first appearance, he stood upon the quarterdeck, staring out over the restless waves. Dressed in black, his figure rose tall and erect as a mighty oak tree. There was a tremendous power about the man, even though his grayish hair and weathered face indicated he could not be much younger than sixty.

I saw no sign of illness, but he did have two vicious marks on him. A long white scar ran along one side of his face, as if he had once been slapped upon the cheek by some terrible force. And one of his legs wasn't a leg at all—it was a piece of polished white whalebone. At once, I realized that false leg of his was the cause of the mysterious clomping.

"'Morning, Captain," I called out, waving a paw. "Weather's warming up a bit, isn't it?"

Captain Ahab glanced at me with icy eyes, saying nothing. I quickly returned to my sweeping. The mere sight of the man made my tail shake.

Chapter Six

The *Pequod* sailed a southeasterly course. After a month, its route began to carry it between the continents of South America and Africa. As the weather gradually warmed, Captain Ahab appeared on deck more and more often. He seldom spoke to anyone, though. He just walked back and forth, gripping the ropes and gunwale to keep himself from stumbling.

thum-Clunk . . . thum-Clunk . . . thum-Clunk . . .

"That can't be easy," the Manxman whispered to me once. "Crossing a pitching deck with only one good leg. I have enough trouble doing it on my *two* legs."

"Me, too," said I. *And I've got* four *legs!* I thought.

Keeping your balance on deck, however, was nowhere near as tricky as doing it a hundred feet high up on the mastheads. These were narrow beams that lay above the uppermost sails on each of the three masts. As I mentioned earlier, we got up there by climbing roped ladders. Indeed, I was doing so much climbing on this voyage, I knew I'd be ready for all those cats when I finally returned ashore. From sunrise to sunset, we took turns standing up on the mastheads. Why is that? We were on the lookout for whale spouts.

I'll explain. You see, even though whales live in the water, they breathe air. They do this through a hole in the top of their head known as a blowhole. The whales rise partially above the water's surface and blow out the old air with a series of spoutings. Other stuff also gushes upward at this time, but no one is really sure if it's water, vapor, or some combination of the two. Then, when the spouting is done, the whale takes a big breath and dives underwater.

Sperm whales, which is what we were searching for, have to come up for air every hour or so. From a high perch atop the ship, the spoutings could be seen for several miles. So there was a fairly good chance we'd spot them if they showed up anywhere near the ship.

"See anything yet?" I called one morning from the mizzenmast to the Icelander on the mainmast.

"Nothing but waves," the Icelander called back. "And they're making me very drowsy."

We weren't really in sperm-whale territory yet, and so far we had not seen any. All the same, I enjoyed my time on the masthead. The breeze up there stroked my coat like a firm brush. I also discovered that a person sees a lot at sea. I watched the gentle curve where water met sky. I studied the colors and contours of the waves. I gazed at unknown birds soaring off to unknown places. Often I caught sight of phantom shapes darting through the water.

And I thought about things. Some of them were minor, but many of them were as deep as the ocean that lay beneath the ship. As I stared thoughtfully at the wide horizon, I couldn't help but feel I was expanding the horizons of my mind. Actually, my thinking often got in the way of my watching.

Everyone's ability to watch, including mine, was sharpened a lot after an important event took place. One evening after supper, Ahab ordered all hands to go up on deck. As the ship rocked with the waves, the captain *thum-Clunked* back and forth a few times. Then he cried out in a voice as bracing as the wind, "What do ye do when ye sight a whale, men?"

"Sing out for him!" all of us shouted.

"Good," Ahab said with a nod. "And what do ye do next, men?"

"Lower the boats and give chase!" we shouted.

"Right," Ahab said with another nod. Then he held a gleaming gold coin in the air. "Look ye! Do ye see this Spanish doubloon? It's a sixteen-dollar piece!"

A murmur swept through the crowd, since that was a sizable sum of money. I found myself calculating how many chew toys it would buy. As the crew watched with great interest, Ahab nailed the coin to the mainmast with a single stroke of a hammer.

"Whosoever of ye first sights a certain sperm whale," Ahab announced, "he shall have this gold coin! Now, listen—the whale I want is like no other ye're likely to see. As ye know, most sperm whales are as gray as an elephant's hide. But this particular whale is white, white, white! White as freshly fallen snow!"

Tashtego, the long-maned Indian harpooner, stepped forward. "Captain Ahab, is this white whale the same that some call Moby Dick?"

It was as if fire flickered in Ahab's eyes. "Aye, Moby Dick! Do ye know the White Whale, then?"

"I think so," Tashtego replied. "Is he quite a bit bigger than most of his kind? And does he have a crookedness to his jaw?"

"Aye, that's him, Tash!"

Dagoo, the black African harpooner, stepped forward. "And does he prowl the seas alone, sir, as do some of the older men whales? And does he also shoot up an especially high spout?"

"Aye, Dagoo!"

Queequeg, my friend the cannibal harpooner, stepped forward. "And does he have one, two, three . . . oh, a good many broken harpoons stuck in his sides? All twisty-twisty, like . . ." Queequeg struggled to come up with the right word.

"Like a corkscrew!" Ahab cried excitedly. "Aye, Queequeg! Aye, by thunder, it's Moby Dick ye three have seen! Do any of the rest of ye know of him?"

The Manxman spoke up. "I've never set eye on this Moby Dick, mind you, but I've heard tell of him. He's become a bit of a legend among some of us sailors. Many a ship

49

has tried to kill him, but none has managed to do it. True, some sperm whales can put up a fight. But when chased, they say, Moby Dick turns back on the boat with a meanness like no other. Indeed, they say he's sent more than a few whaling men down to a wet and salty grave."

The Chinese man spoke. "I hear say this whale might be as much as two hundred years old. I also hear say he might be old as time itself. Because he keeps on living after being struck at so often."

The Brazilian spoke. "Some sailors swear this whale has attacked two different ships in two different places far away from each other at the exact same moment!"

My long lower jaw opened with wonder. Whalemen are given to telling tall tales, so I doubted some of these reports. Yet, this Moby Dick aroused my curiosity. It obviously aroused far more in Ahab.

He clomped along so excitedly that he barely kept his balance. "Aye, men!" he cried with blazing eyes. "He's the demon of the seas! I'll warn ye, he's crafty as they come. So ye'll have to keep yer eyes peeled sharp as daggers. But I promise it'll be worth the effort. For, if all goes well, we'll be killing the most wicked and malicious creature that ever lived! Moby Dick! Moby Dick! Moby Dick!"

We all stood silent, not sure what to make of Ahab's strange display of passion. Finally, Starbuck, the responsible chief mate, spoke. "Captain Ahab, was it Moby Dick that took off your leg?"

Ahab stopped and ran a hand along his whalebone leg. "Aye," he whispered bitterly. "It was Moby Dick that brought me to this dead stump I stand on now. Aye, Moby Dick. And I'll chase him around all sides of the earth before I give him up. And this is what ye have gone to sea for, men. This alone is our true mission—to chase that blasted White Whale until he spouts black blood!"

I gave my side a scratch with one of my back paws. *Actually, this was* not *what we went out to sea for,* I thought. I could also see that Starbuck was troubled by this news. Ahab noticed it, too.

"What's that long face about, Mr. Starbuck?" he asked. "Art thou not game for Moby Dick?"

"Sir," Starbuck said evenly, "I am game for any whale if it comes in the way of business; in the way of gathering oil to sell on the market. Business is what me and the rest are here for, sir—not our commander's chance to seek revenge."

Ahab eyed Starbuck a moment. "Fearest not," he said with a growl. "I'll give thee thy oily business. We'll squeeze some cold cash out of all the men's lays. Aye, we shall hunt any blasted sperm whale we've time and opportunity for. But it's Moby Dick we're after most. Because, I tell thee, this murderous white monster is a threat to the world!"

"No." Starbuck spoke louder. "He is only a beast. A simple whale that struck you out of nothing but blind instinct. You and your crew attacked him with weapons, and the whale lashed back at you to protect himself!"

"That's not the truth!" Ahab roared like a lion. "I see beneath the mask of things, and I know what I know!"

Starbuck kept himself from arguing further, well aware it was a bad idea to disagree with the captain.

Ahab turned from Starbuck to the other men and cried out, "What say ye, men? Are ye brave enough for the task at hand?"

"Huzza! Huzza! Huzza!" the men cheered loudly. That was their way of saying *yes, yes, yes.* Caught up in the excitement of the moment, I confess—I, too, barked out my approval. Perhaps there was some sort of magic in Ahab's fiery eyes. I'm not sure. But, for whatever reason, every man except Starbuck seemed to swallow with gusto Ahab's hatred of this White Whale.

The captain ordered the serving-boy to fetch a cask of grog and several large mugs. As the grog was poured forth, Ahab had the men form a human circle around him.

"Let us drink to our pledge!" Ahab cried to the sky. "Death to Moby Dick! By thunder, we shall hunt the White Whale until he spouts black blood! Drink and pass! Round and round with it! Long swallows, and bless ye!"

The men passed the mugs and drank greedily, much of the liquor splashing down their faces. After Queequeg took a drink, he set a mug on the deck for me. I stuck my muzzle inside, took a sniff, then lapped up a few licks. Myself, I'm mostly a water drinker. The grog, which was made of a foul-smelling rum, burned my belly as if it was sulfur.

"Where do they get this stuff?" I gasped.

A little later, some other crew members and I relaxed around the deck. Darkness fell and the breeze of a cool trade-wind stroked my fur as if it were a gentle hand. Again Queequeg shared his pipe with Tashtego and Dagoo. The Spaniard lay on a coil of rope, snoring loudly as a snorting bull.

The American spoke as he worked with a knife to carve a picture on a whale's tooth the size of my head. "I met a man who sailed on Ahab's last voyage. He says Ahab came face to face with Moby Dick while standing in the bow of a broken rowboat. All the harpoons and lances were gone, so Ahab stabbed at the whale with nothing but a six-inch dagger blade. Well, sir, that whale ripped away Ahab's leg the way a farmer cuts away wheat in a field. On the journey home, the sailor claims, Ahab was raving like a madman. Both his body and mind throbbing with pain. They had to tie him down to his bed most of the journey. And yet, by the time they reached

Nantucket, the captain seemed well enough. A bit changed, perhaps, but . . . well enough."

The Dutchman tiredly rubbed his face. "Ach, so what if he's a little wild. Whaling's a wild profession. I say he's the best of captains, and maybe all the better for having a measure of rage."

The Sicilian spat on the deck. "I believe the same."

I had been chewing on a stray piece of rope as I listened. Now I threw in my opinion. "You know what bothers me about this Ahab character? That irritating clomping every night. I wake up thinking the man is trampling on my face. Isn't there some way he could muffle that whalebone leg? Perhaps with a bunch of rags or—"

Sensing someone behind me, I turned. My whiskers twitched. Ahab stood there, scowling down at me.

"Avast!" he snarled with a show of teeth. "Is a common sailor like you giving orders to the likes of me?"

I nervously tried to tuck my tail between my legs. "Uh . . . no, sir. I wasn't speaking of you. Actually . . . I was speaking of another captain I sailed with. He also had a whalebone leg. Or, no . . . now that I think of it, his leg was made of elephant tusk. Yes, that's right. It was carved from elephant tusk. Which is much more bothersome than . . . uh . . . whalebone."

Ahab showed the faintest trace of a smile. "I should not have spoken to ye so harsh. My apologies. One day, young lad, I shall be counting on thy courage."

He gave my back a brief rub, then clomped steadily away. Though the man was far from friendly, he gave off something similar to a magnetic effect. Like the iron needle of a compass, I found myself strangely drawn to him.

Before going to bed that night, I crept down the quarterdeck hatchway, careful not to let my nails click too much. I paused outside the captain's cabin. The door was slightly open. I saw Ahab sitting at a table, several yellowed sea charts spread out before him. As he drew a line with a pencil, a lantern swung from the ceiling, swaying with the ship's motion.

Somehow I just knew Ahab was plotting a course to find Moby Dick. In general, sperm whales can be found with some reliability. Though they travel all over the globe, they tend to spend certain seasons in certain waters. Yet, finding *one particular whale . . .* well, that was another matter. I figured our chances of crossing paths with this one creature were almost impossible.

It seemed Ahab didn't agree with me. He dropped his pencil and muttered, "I shall find thee, Moby Dick, if my men and I have to plunge through every fathom of the world's water. I care not for profit. Nor caution. Only thee."

If old Peleg and Bildad could see this, I thought, their hair would probably turn even whiter than it was. Perhaps mine would, too, before this voyage was done.

Having fun? Sure, I thought so. Well, as the *Pequod* sails on in search of Moby Dick, let's see how the gang back home does with their Internet search. Hey, maybe we can also pick up a quick snack. Adventure tends to make me very hungry.

Chapter Seven

David tapped keys at his computer, the screen glowing in front of him. Wishbone knew the boy was somehow diving into that mysterious place called the Internet. "Okay, now we just wait a few seconds," David said as he unwrapped a small piece of coconut candy.

Everyone was in David's room. Joe and Sam stood behind David's chair, while Wishbone jumped on a chair right beside David.

"Hey there," Wishbone said, eyes attached to the piece of candy. "How's it going, my old friend? I see you've got something to eat there in your hand. Mmm, smells awfully nice."

David started to take a bite of the candy. But then a page jumped onto the screen, and David tapped more keys. "I'm checking to see if Wilson High has a home page," he explained.

"Say, if it's not too much trouble," Wishbone said casually, "I might like a bite of that thing myself."

Moments later, a new page jumped onto the screen. "Yeah, here it is," David said, setting down the piece of

candy. "The Wilson High School Home Page. Let's see if they've got a section on sports. . . . Yes, they do."

David clicked his mouse and another page jumped onto the screen. By that time, Wishbone had completely eaten the coconut candy and was licking his lips. "Thanks," he told David. "You're too generous. Really."

"Here we go," David said, using his mouse to scroll down the screen. "Basketball is right on top."

With his front paws on the desk, Wishbone watched a bunch of letters rise magically upward. "These computers are incredible, aren't they?" Wishbone said to the others. "Perhaps the single greatest advance for Man and Dog in the twentieth century."

On the screen, several color photographs appeared. "Stop! That's him!" Joe cried, pointing.

Wishbone peered closer. One picture showed the very same hefty high-school boy who had stolen Joe's basketball. He wore a dark blue basketball uniform with the number "32" in white. The boy was dribbling downcourt with a determined look in his eyes. He led with one shoulder almost like a football player running up the middle of the field.

Wishbone turned to Joe, who was also studying the picture. Joe liked most everyone he met, but·Wishbone could see that Joe did not like the looks of this number-32 fellow at all. *And why should he?* Wishbone thought. *Let's not forget, this is the guy who made off with the basketball Joe's father gave him when he was six years old. If anything is a reason for dislike, that would be it.*

"Look at him," Joe said in a low voice. "I think Damont was right. This guy looks mean as they come. Check out those eyes. He's just daring anyone to get near him."

"Yeah," Wishbone agreed. "Not only does he look like a bulldog, he looks like a bad-guy bulldog. You know, I knew a bulldog once who—"

"To me it just looks like he's concentrating," Sam remarked. "Joe, I think you might be jumping to some conclusions about this guy because of what he did to you. It's understandable, but . . . Let's wait a bit before making up our minds."

"And let's get some factual information," David said, scrolling farther down the page. He moved past a few more names. "Okay, here's the team roster."

Wishbone tilted his head. "I can't quite read it. I have a little trouble with these computer screens. Too much glare."

"Let's see," Joe said, leaning in toward the screen. "Number Thirty-two. There it is. Aha! His name is Richard Everson! He's even got a mean-sounding name."

"Joe, you're being silly," Sam pointed out. "Richard Everson is a perfectly normal name."

"Richard Everson," Joe said quietly as the screen's glow reflected off his face. "Richard Everson. Richard Everson."

David scrolled down farther, stopping at a list of names and numbers. "Here's the stats for all the players," he said. "Let's check out Everson. Wow! He's pretty good. He leads the team in both scores and rebounds. In one game he made twenty-six points."

"Hey, look," Sam said, pointing. "There's a footnote under the statistics. It says, 'Starting April 20, Richard Everson will be temporarily out of action.' Maybe he's injured."

"He's not injured," Joe said, moving away from the desk. "He looked just fine to me an hour ago. The guy's obviously been suspended from the team. And I'll bet you anything I know why—unsportsmanlike conduct!"

"Aren't there other reasons why a player could be suspended?" David asked.

"Look, it's plain as day," Joe said emphatically. "You can see how mean he looks in that photo. And if that's not enough, how about the way he swiped my basketball? There's no two ways about it. That was a mean thing to do!"

"True," Sam admitted.

David hit a key, and a computerized voice said, "See ya later, David."

David swiveled in his chair to face Joe and said, "Well, now we know the guy's name. The question is: What are we going to do next?"

Sam squinted, as if thinking. "I'm not quite sure," she said. "Maybe we could find his phone number and give him a call. Or maybe we should write him a letter. We could explain the importance of that particular basketball. Who knows? The guy may end up feeling terrible about the whole thing."

Joe began to pace the room, clenching and unclenching his fist. "I'm not so sure about that. If this guy is really so mean, he won't care about me or my dad."

"Joe," Sam said with a worried look, "you're not still thinking of going after this guy, are you?"

"No, I guess not," Joe answered.

Uh-oh . . . Wishbone thought. *That didn't sound very convincing to me.*

"I'm not sure I believe you," Sam said, going over to Joe. "Look, even if this boy was suspended for unsportsmanlike conduct, which we don't know for sure, that's no reason to confront him."

"In fact," David said from the desk, "it's all the more reason *not* to confront him. If he's half as mean as you think he is, he could try to hurt you. I'm serious, Joe."

"All right, all right," Joe said, holding up a hand. "I get the idea!"

"Good," Sam said. "I'll tell you what. Let's all give this some serious thought and see what we can come up with. We'll figure something out. I guarantee it, Joe, we'll find a way to get the basketball back."

"Okay," David said, standing up. "Now, I'd better kick you guys out of here. I've got to fix my mother's vacuum cleaner. Then I've got to start working on my book report. . . . Hey, who ate my candy?"

"Not me," Sam said, with a sly glance at Wishbone. "But now that you mention it, I'd better start on my book report, too. Have you started yours, Joe?"

"No," Joe said, still pacing.

"Well, you'd better get to it," Sam advised. "Remember, they're due on Monday. Wishbone, David and I are depending on you to make sure Joe gets home to do his schoolwork. Got it?"

"You can count on me," Wishbone said as Sam gave his head a quick scratch.

David went over to Joe and put a hand on his shoulder. "And Joe, promise us you won't go looking for this Everson guy. Also, promise us you won't do anything about this situation without first discussing it with me and Sam."

Joe huffed in irritation. "Okay, I promise. Are you guys happy now?"

"Yes," David and Sam said together.

But Wishbone saw something they didn't see— namely, that Joe had two fingers crossed behind his back. *I don't approve of this dishonesty,* Wishbone thought, *but I'll keep quiet about it. A true dog never rats on his best friend.*

Joe motioned to Wishbone. "Come on, boy, let's hit the road."

Something about the way he said it made Wishbone buzz with both nervousness and excitement. He knew Joe very well, and he could tell they were about to go off in search of Richard Everson. Right then. What he didn't know was what Joe planned to do if and when they actually found this guy.

Wishbone leaped to the floor and said, "As always, ready when you are, Joe!"

Look, if you want adventure, you have to be willing to take a risk now and then. I just hope Joe and I are not taking too big of a risk—nothing as risky, say, as the situation Ishmael and his mates are about to face. Hang on for a whale of a ride!

Wishbone's Basic Guide to Whales and Whaling

Before we actually meet up with a whale,
we ought to arm ourselves with
some information.

barb   the sharp triangular tip at the head of a harpoon

blowhole   the hole on top of the whale's head used for breathing air

blubber   a layer of fat right beneath the whale's tough outer skin

breach   when a whale leaps out of the water and "breaks" through the surface

fathom   a unit of length that is used to measure the depth of water (1 fathom equals 6 feet)

flukes   the two flat fins at the tip of the whale's tail

harpoon   a long, spearlike weapon that is hurled at a whale. The front end of the harpoon has a sharpened point called a barb. The back end of the harpoon is attached to a sturdy rope that allows the whalers to pull themselves up to the whale.

lance   a spear used for killing whales, mostly at close range

lash
to bind or tie tightly with rope. Captured whales were often lashed to the side of the main vessel until the crew could get it aboard to drain it of its oil.

sound
when a whale dives down suddenly through the water

sperm whale
the second largest kind of whale. (The largest is the blue whale, which can weigh more than two hundred tons—400,000 pounds—and be longer than a jet airplane!) Sperm whales were especially valuable in the nineteenth century because they were filled with tremendous amounts of oil and spermaceti (hang on—this one is coming right up!). The vast majority of sperm whales are gray, but every once in a while there is a white one.

spermaceti
an oily substance found in the head of the sperm whale. The finest candles in the world were once made from it.

whale
a broad category of sea-living mammal. (In Melville's day, whales were considered fish, but this is no longer the case.) There are about eighty living species of whales, including dolphins and porpoises. The larger whales are the biggest creatures that ever lived—yes, that means even bigger than the biggest dinosaurs.

whale oil
an oil obtained from a whale by boiling its blubber. It used to be a popular fuel for oil lamps and lanterns.

Chapter Eight

Following Ahab's charts, the *Pequod* began swooping around the southern tip of Africa. There, where the Atlantic Ocean joins the Indian Ocean, lies a stretch of water known as the Cape of Good Hope. It's a terrible name for the place. There's nothing "good" or "hopeful" about it. The Cape's green waves are always angry, and when they throw a tantrum, it comes in the shape of a ship-demolishing storm. I kept my keen nose on full alert for the scent of bad weather.

Dangerous as the area is, many sperm whales cruise through this rich feeding ground. Therefore, every man kept especially watchful, knowing we would very soon catch sight of our first whale. And so we did.

Late one afternoon, Tashtego, the Indian, was standing watch and he sounded out a wildly musical cry. "There she blows! There! There! There she blows!"

At once, everyone flew into action, pulling at ropes and climbing the rope ladders to adjust the ivory-colored sails. Within seconds, the *Pequod* was bearing down on the spoutings that Tashtego had sighted.

"A whole school of them there!" shouted Dagoo, the

African, as he watched from the bow. "Maybe twenty in all! There's no Moby there, but, by the spouts, I see they be sperm whales for sure!"

Using my claws, I climbed up into the rigging to get a better look. Amid the distant waves, I saw a number of upward gushes that reminded me of decorative fountains in a wealthy family's garden. A sharp wind filled our sails, and we quickly drew closer to the spoutings.

Ahab stood on the quarterdeck, viewing the whales through a telescope. Finally, he shouted, "Lower the boats!"

I leaped to the deck and flew on all fours for the larboard gunwale. A whaling vessel keeps a collection of cedarwood rowboats hanging over its sides, and we began cranking three of them downward. Just as my boat hit the water, a sailor cried out, "Who the devil is that?"

I turned to see five unfamiliar sailors, who began cranking down a fourth boat under Ahab's supervision. "Pay no heed to them," Ahab ordered the rest of us. "They are my private team!"

I realized these men were the shadowy shapes I had seen boarding the ship that first day. They were stowaways—unsigned passengers hidden on the ship. Ahab had sneaked them aboard because he didn't want the boat's owners to know he was planning on manning a rowboat himself. Captains seldom took part in the whale chase because there was too great a risk they would lose their life. Of course, Ahab was not your regular captain.

There was no time to stare at the stowaways. It was time for a whale chase. Most of us climbed over the gunwales, dropped into the four boats, and away we rowed. Though a little nervous, I was mostly looking forward to this part of the job. I had always enjoyed chasing things, especially cats and fast-moving vehicles.

"Stroke, my good men!" Starbuck, the chief mate, called out with authority. "That's it, lads, that's it! Long and steady! Stroke!"

Ahab, Starbuck, Stubb, and Flask commanded the boats, each of which contained a total of six men. The commanders steered from the stern, while the rest of us sat facing them, our backs to the bow. Queequeg and I were both assigned to Starbuck's boat. Seated on a plank bench, I gripped an oar between my front paws and pulled it repeatedly through the Cape's rough waters.

"Ishmael, are you afraid?" Starbuck called out to me. "This being your first time 'going on the whale,' as they say."

"No, sir," I answered.

"Tell the truth, lad."

"Well, perhaps just a tiny bit."

"Good," Starbuck replied. "I don't want any man in my boat who's not afraid of a whale. It's not cowardice, it's caution."

The boat of Stubb, the second mate, hurried along to one side of us. "Pull, pull, pull, ye ragamuffins!" Stubb scolded his crew in his comical fashion. "Stop snoring, boys, and pull, will ye? Just keep thinking of that juicy whale steak! Pull, boys, pull!"

The boat of Flask, the third mate, hurried along on the other side of us. "Row, men, row!" Flask instructed his crew in a matter-of-fact manner. "Fear not. A whale is nothing but an oversized mouse! Row, men, row! Row, men, row!"

I saw Ahab's boat skimming over the waves, soaring ahead of the others. The captain spoke not a word, but he didn't need to. His stowaway crew was obviously very skilled at their seafaring task.

The harpooners sat in the front of each boat, and they each sent out a primitive cry as they rowed.

"Woo-hoo! Wa-hee!" Tashtego whooped.

"Ke-hee! Kee-hee!" Dagoo bellowed.

"Ka-la! Ka-loo!" Queequeg howled.

With every stroke of my oar, my tail thumped with anticipation. I was finally about to see a whale, the world's most mammoth and magnificent creature!

Suddenly Starbuck raised a hand, and we lifted our oars, slowing the boat to a drift. I turned around to see that the whales had disappeared underwater. This might have been because they were done with their spouting, in which case they would be gone for a while. Or it might have been because they were frightened by us, in which case they would have to resurface soon to finish their breathing process.

Queequeg stood, scanning the waves. Flask went up front and made Dagoo lift him up on his broad shoulders. Tashtego tilted his head to try to hear a sigh of the whales. I pricked up my own ears.

Up ahead I caught a quick look of Ahab's harpooner. He was a slender man wearing a wide-brimmed hat. The fellow stood so tall and straight that he could have been a harpoon himself.

Moments later, I heard something somewhere in the sea. Tashtego pointed silently to the right. I looked. Not far away, bubbles and wisps of vapor appeared on the water's surface. Suddenly a fountain burst into the air. It scared the wits out of me. Even though I was close, I still couldn't tell if it was water, mist, or steam being spouted.

Then, beneath the spout, I glimpsed the upper portion of a whale. The body stretched out gigantically long, its smoky-gray surface glistening with slickness. I noticed a very wide, squarish head, a swell of hump somewhere in the middle, and a hint of tail at the end.

I spotted another whale nearby. Then another. Then

several more. Every one of them shot off their spouts as they glided half atop the waves with surprising grace. Because we were no longer rowing, the whales were happily unaware of our presence.

Not for long, though. As Ahab gestured, the crews of all four boats turned away from the whales to grip their oars. Starbuck pointed and our crew began rowing in the indicated direction. I noticed the other boats moving away from one another so each boat could attack its own separate whale.

"Stroke, men, stroke!" Starbuck called, acting as the eyes for our boat. "The whale sees us now, poor fellow. He's running with all his might, leaving a trail of frightened white water in his wake. Put yer backs into it, men! Come on. That's it. We're pulling closer . . . closer . . . yes, we're almost . . . Now, Queequeg! Stand and give it to him!"

Still rowing, I whipped around to watch. Balancing like an acrobat, Queequeg stood at the bow of the rushing boat. He raised high his harpoon, took quick aim, and hurled the weapon through the air as if throwing a stick for someone to fetch. The harpoon's sharpened barb stuck in the whale's gray hump.

The whale jerked away, then thrashed about, churning up an earthquake of waves. The harpoon was not designed to kill the whale. It was simply part of our method of getting close to the creature. We stopped rowing, but our boat now tumbled and tossed, water splashing up at us.

As the whale rolled partly on its side, I caught a better look at its head. I gasped at the size and strangeness of it. The head of a sperm whale is a very large mass of blank space that runs for one-third of the whale's body. The only features are a mouth, way at the bottom, and tiny black eyes, way at the back on either side. In fact, the eyes are so far apart from each other that the whale sees two

totally different views. A shudder ran through my fur as I realized this whale could swallow me as easily as I swallow a fallen scrap from the table!

Suddenly the whale righted itself and swam through the waves with great speed. He kept his head partly above water as he fled, which seemed to help the whale move its fastest.

A rope whizzed through metal grooves near my paws. The end of the rope was attached to the harpoon that was stuck in the whale; the rest of it uncoiled from a barrel sitting in the boat's stern. The rope traveled so fast it actually hissed and smoked. I was careful to stay clear of the rope, knowing it could catch hold of me and drag me right out of the boat and downward into the roughened sea.

Soon our boat jumped and we were being pulled through the water along with the swiftly fleeing whale. "Gentlemen," Starbuck told us, "they call this a Nantucket sleigh ride! Somebody wet the line, please!"

The Frenchman filled his cap with seawater, which he threw on the sizzling rope. This was done to keep the rope from bursting into flames.

"Switch!" Starbuck called after several minutes of flight. Then he and Queequeg changed places. This was an incredibly difficult job, considering the speed of the boat and the roughness of the waves. There was a reason for it, though. The whale would be tiring soon, and when he did, Starbuck would be plunging a sharpened lance into the whale, thus killing him.

But this whale didn't feel like following the plan. Suddenly his immense tail flew in the air, and I caught sight of the two flattened fins at the tip. These are known as flukes. My own tail quivered as I noticed that each fluke was as tall as a man. Then the whale's tail disappeared into the waves.

"He's sounding!" the man from Portugal cried with alarm. The rope whizzed out of the barrel even faster.

Seeing my confusion, the Frenchman quickly told me, "That means he's diving down very fast. Perhaps a mile deep. Some say that's why the sperm whale has so much oil in his head. It may help the weight to shift around so the whale can swim more speedily. But no one knows if this really be true. We just hope the whale won't—"

The rope jerked to a stop, tight as a harp string. The next instant, the boat's stern swung into the air, spilling us out of our seats.

"He's pulling us down!" the Tahitian yelled.

I clamped my jaws together, afraid we might die any second.

"We can pull him other way!" Queequeg called, heaving on the rope with his muscular arms. "I think-ee we can!"

"Perhaps," Starbuck said, getting up to examine the tightly stretched rope. "Or perhaps he'll yank us all down to a watery death. It's far too risky for my liking." Starbuck sliced through the rope with a dagger. Immediately, the stern of the boat bounced down as the whale dove deeper to freedom.

I opened my locked jaws, breathing with relief.

"Plenty more whales out there," Starbuck told us. "Let us assist Mr. Stubb. I believe the ol' joker and his men are fast closing in on a whale just up yonder."

We rowed our way to Stubb's boat, where his men had been more successful than we had. Each man hauled at his rope, the far end of which was attached by harpoon to an exhausted whale. Soon they had the boat right alongside the whale, which continued towing the boat slowly forward.

Balancing at the bow, Stubb lifted a lance, which was similar to a harpoon, but smaller. Stubb drove the lance into the whale's slippery gray skin. Thick blood spurted out, soon rolling like a river down the whale's side. The whale thrashed in pain, violently swinging its tail flukes. Around the stricken whale the water turned into a boiling caldron of white foam.

"Pull up! Pull up!" Stubb ordered. The men kept pulling on the rope until the boat was actually out of the water and balancing on the whale's back. Stubb leaned over and drove the lance into the whale's blowhole, which was toward the front of the head. Stubb dug the lance in deeper, then ground it around with a circular motion. Gradually losing strength, the whale rolled from side to side, struggling to live.

Feeling great pity for the whale, I covered my eyes with a paw. When I looked a few minutes later, the majestic creature lay dead.

I ran my eyes along the whale's floating body. The sheer hugeness of it took my breath away. Next to the blue whale, the sperm whale is the most gigantic animal that ever lived. I had been told some of them grew to a length of eighty feet and weighed ninety tons—180,000 pounds—but it was quite another matter to view up close a beast almost as big as a ship!

"'Afternoon, Mr. Starbuck," Stubb called with a cheerful wave. "Perhaps you'll be so kind as to help us haul this blubbery fellow back to our home away from home!"

Using ropes, both boats hauled the colossal creature through the water. Soon the *Pequod* met us halfway. This whale turned out to be the only one we had caught on this chase, but a single sperm whale contained so much oil that we considered the day a complete success. Before long the whale was tied alongside the ship's hull, and everyone fell to the deck with fatigue. I felt as if I'd been chasing my tail in circles for hours on end.

"Queequeg," I said to my friend, who lay beside me, "this whaling game is a dangerous business. Perhaps we should have gone fishing for lobsters instead."

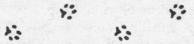

After several days and a storm that slapped us around pretty good, we said farewell to the Cape of Good Hope. The *Pequod* sailed a northeasterly course through the Indian Ocean, moving toward the lower part of Asia. In those waters, we chased and killed two more sperm whales. By that time, Ahab's stowaway crew mixed with the rest of us a little bit, but not much. I never learned exactly why Ahab had kept them hidden so long, but the man worked in strange ways.

After a while, the ship reversed into a southerly course, eventually skimming along near the Indonesian islands of Sumatra, Java, and Bali. But don't think that we ever stopped to have a look at the spices, jewels, or buried bones of those exotic islands. Indeed, at no time on this journey did we ever draw close enough to shore for anything but the slighest glimpse of tree or sand.

One night, as we neared Australia, we spotted an especially high spout shining in the moonlight. Even though it was dark, the *Pequod* gave chase. But the spout did not reappear. This was unusual, because whales almost always blew their spouts repeatedly, often with such regularity you could set a clock by them.

Every couple of nights, the same event occurred. Finally, we realized it wouldn't be possible to catch this whale—at least not in the darkness. Although he never said so, I could see from Ahab's sharp gaze that he believed the spout may have belonged to Moby Dick.

On a tropically warm night around this time, I stood at the bow with my front paws on the gunwale. Queequeg walked up to me and asked, "Watch-ee for the spout?"

"Yes," I replied. "Do you think it might be Moby Dick?"

Queequeg shrugged. "Perhaps. Perhaps not."

"I never thought we would find him. But perhaps we did."

"Or perhaps he found us."

"Whoever this whale might be, it's like he's playing a trick on us. He could be drawing us forward so he can attack us at the place of his choosing. I've known some cats who used that kind of tactic."

"Perhaps. But then . . . perhaps not."

I scratched the underside of my muzzle. "You know, Queequeg, I'm the type who likes to fully understand matters. But these whales are so mysterious. There's so much we don't know about them: how deep they dive; how they catch their food; why they carry all that oil in their head. We don't even know what that stuff they spout is made of."

"Perhaps we not supposed to know everything," Queequeg said, calm as a clam. He ruffled the back of my neck affectionately. Then he wandered away to smoke his pipe with the other two harpooners.

I stood alone, watching the dark water ahead. I found my thoughts haunted by this Moby Dick. Perhaps it was his color. A white whale is a very rare thing in nature. Also, I find no other color has quite the same power to affect our souls.

Many of the world's most treasured objects are white, from shiny pearls to the beautiful marble statues carved by the likes of Michelangelo. Brides wear white for the innocence it symbolizes, and the white dove is seen as a symbol of peace and hope.

Sorry to interrupt. But let me just add that the Iroquois, a Native American tribe, consider white dogs to be sacred! Okay, carry on.

Yet, many of the most terrifying sights are also white. Few creatures are feared as much as the white polar bear of the North Pole, or the white shark of the Tropics. That most scary of all visions, the ghost, is usually thought to have a pale white face and wear flowing white garments; often, it is pictured rising from a vapory white fog.

I thought back to my visit at the chapel in New Bedford. I remembered Father Mapple's sermon, and how he said that everything in the universe held many meanings. I realized that would certainly apply to that most mysterious of colors, white. And those words might also apply to the most mysterious of all whales— Moby Dick.

Only moments later, I glimpsed the spout once again. By the moon's glow, the upward gush glimmered an eerie yet also heavenly shade of silvery-white.

I told you this was a great tale, didn't I? And, just wait, the farther away from home these guys travel, the more interesting things get. Which reminds me— Joe and I are traveling farther away from home, too. We're off in search of the guy who stole Joe's basketball.

Chapter Nine

"Have you seen a big teenage boy wearing a dark blue school jacket?" Joe asked. "He was probably carrying a basketball." He and Wishbone were standing in front of the Oakdale Public Library speaking to one of the mail carriers, Mr. Bloodgood.

The mail carrier tapped his fingers on the handle of his mail cart. "Blue school jacket . . . basketball . . . Nope, doesn't ring a bell. Sorry, Joe."

"Okay, thanks," Joe said with a wave.

He and Wishbone began to move down Main Street. After leaving David's house, Joe had looked up Richard Everson's phone number and called, but there was no answer. Then he and Wishbone had traveled the few short blocks to downtown Oakdale, where they hoped to pick up Everson's trail. Most of the town's shops, restaurants, and offices were located there, but the area was less crowded than usual. Wishbone figured that was because a few dark clouds remained overhead, threatening a return of the rain.

Though he and Joe hadn't discussed it, Wishbone knew exactly what Joe was up to. Joe figured Richard

Everson might still be in the Oakdale area, and he wanted to find him. As soon as possible.

A bit farther down the street, Wishbone saw a familiar figure come out from the Oakdale *Chronicle* building. It was Wanda Gilmore, the Talbots' neighbor who owned the town's newspaper.

"Hi, Miss Gilmore," Joe said, as he and Wishbone approached. "How's it going?"

"Well, they have a crisis with the paper," Wanda said with gesturing hands. "It seems there's absolutely no news happening today. That means we have nothing to put in tomorrow's edition!"

"Stick around," Wishbone joked. "'Boy and His Dog Attacked by High School Whale' ought to make for an interesting headline."

"I have one quick question," Joe said to Wanda. "Have you seen a big teenage boy in a dark blue school jacket?"

Wanda scrunched her face, thinking. "Gosh, I don't think I have, Joe. Sorry."

"Thanks anyway," Joe said. Then he immediately moved down the street, with Wishbone following alongside him.

As Wishbone walked with Joe, he thought, *Joe's not spending as much time chatting with people as he usually does. And he isn't showing his smile at all. In fact, he seems to be wearing a sort of frown on his face, the kind he gets when he's at the end of his rope with his math homework. Poor guy. He's really upset about losing that ball.*

"Hey, Joe!" a voice called.

Wishbone and Joe both turned around to see Gavin running toward them. He was a skinny boy from Joe's grade at school. With both hands, Gavin was hauling a very large shopping bag.

"What's up?" Joe asked, as Gavin drew to a stop in front of him.

"I'm glad I found you," Gavin said, catching his breath. "I went by your house, but you weren't home."

"Why did you go by my house?" Joe asked.

"You were supposed to help me today," Gavin said.

Joe looked confused. "Help you with what?"

"Don't you remember?" Gavin said, setting down the bag. "Last week I got a bunch of birthday money. Even though I'm not a very good baseball player, I decided I'd buy some really nice equipment, thinking maybe that would help me to get better. But I got a little carried away in the store and ended up buying a full set of catcher's equipment. After I got this stuff home, I realized I don't want to be a catcher. He spends half of the game getting a ball thrown right at him!"

Wishbone peered inside the bag, seeing a mask and protective devices for every single part of the body. "Catcher isn't my favorite position, either," he commented.

Joe slapped his forehead. "Yeah, now I remember. You wanted to exchange the catcher's gear for a really

good fielder's mitt, and then you'd spend the leftover money on something else. And I said I'd go to the store with you and make sure you got the best mitt."

"Right," Gavin said, nodding with enthusiasm. "And we agreed to do it this afternoon."

"I'm really sorry," Joe said. "I forgot all about it."

"Me, too," Wishbone put in. "Joe, we've got to start writing down our appointments."

Gavin gave a shrug. "Well, no harm done. I found you anyway, so we can do it right now."

An awkward moment passed. Finally, Joe said, "Gavin, I can't. I'm kind of busy right now."

"It shouldn't take long," Gavin said. "And I could really use your help. You're the best athlete I know."

Joe put a hand on Gavin's shoulder. Wishbone could tell he felt bad about bailing out on his schoolmate.

"Gavin, it's just a really bad day for me," Joe said. "I'll be happy to do it another day, or, if you can't wait, I'm sure they'll be able to help you at the store. Believe me, I feel terrible about this, but . . . I'm just right in the middle of something very important."

Gavin nodded with disappointment. "Okay, I guess I understand. See ya later."

Gavin picked up his overloaded bag of catcher's equipment and walked away. As Joe watched him head off, Wishbone got the impression Joe was trying to decide whether or not he should run after Gavin and spend some time helping him, after all. Apparently Joe decided against this course of action. He turned and continued on his way, moving in the opposite direction from where Gavin was going.

Joe's definitely not acting like himself, Wishbone thought as he followed Joe. *He's always willing to help a fellow kid in need. I guess he just can't think of anything else but that stolen ball. Which is certainly understandable. All the same, he's making me really nervous for some reason. Maybe it's the way he keeps clenching and unclenching his fist.*

Joe and Wishbone turned onto another street. In front of the bank, Joe stopped to talk with Officer Krulla, one of Oakdale's handful of uniformed police officers.

"Howdy, Joe," Officer Krulla greeted.

"Hi," Joe replied quickly. "Did you happen to see a big blond teenage boy wearing a dark blue school jacket?"

Officer Krulla pushed back his cap. "A big blond fellow? And was it a jacket from Wilson High School?"

"Yeah—that's him!" Joe said excitedly.

"Matter of fact, I *did* see him. He was at the basketball court in Jackson Park."

"When did you see him there?"

"Oh, maybe ten minutes ago. Is there anything I can help—"

"Thanks a lot," Joe said, hurrying off in the opposite direction.

Wishbone glanced at Officer Krulla, then ran to catch up with Joe. "Hey, Joe. Maybe we should go back there and tell Officer Krulla what's going on. He might be able to help us get that basketball back. Officers of the law can be very helpful when it comes to dealing with reckless members of society."

Joe kept walking at a swift pace. Wishbone ran alongside.

"Joe, look," Wishbone continued. "I really think it might be a good idea for us to bring Officer Krulla to the park with us. He's got a shiny badge and all kinds of neat things on his belt and—"

Joe plunged onward. Wishbone slowed down, realizing Joe wasn't the least bit interested in his advice.

Now I understand what's making me nervous, Wishbone thought. *It seems Joe's getting a little out of control here. He doesn't want the help of Officer Krulla or anyone else. It's almost as if he's more interested in facing off with this Everson fellow than he is in actually getting the ball back. Which means Joe is likely to say or do something rash when he and Everson finally meet up. And that could be a major problem!*

Wishbone stopped walking.

Joe, who was now a half block ahead, realized Wishbone was no longer beside him. He turned around and called, "Wishbone, come on, boy. He's at the basketball court in the park. We need to get there before he leaves!"

Wishbone stood in place. "Joe, I've been thinking about this and . . . I know you want that ball back, and so do I. But we might be going about this the wrong way. Remember, this Everson character is big. As in *real big*. And if we're not careful, he could flatten us into a pair of pancakes!"

"What are you waiting for?" Joe called impatiently.

"I'm waiting for you to return to your senses," Wishbone replied. "I told Sam and David I'd watch out for you, and that's exactly what I'm doing. The bottom line is, we've got no business messing around with this guy, and you know it!"

"I'm still waiting," Joe called.

"So am I," Wishbone said, sitting down.

"Fine," Joe snapped with a rare show of anger. "I'll just go to the park without you. Find your own way home!"

Wishbone watched Joe turn and stalk away. Joe almost never yelled at Wishbone, and it pained the dog deeply when it did happen. Even so, Wishbone knew what he had to do.

I have no choice but to follow him, Wishbone thought.

Even when I'm not wearing a leash, it's like there's an invisible leash binding me to Joe. Why? He's my best buddy in the entire world. Wherever he goes, I go, too. No matter what. Besides, if things get as ugly as I think they might, Joe will need me there to protect him. Okay, here goes nothing.

Wishbone sprang to his feet and trotted after Joe. But every instinct in his body warned him that they were headed straight for the jaws of danger.

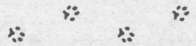

You know, the relationship between a master and dog can be a lot like the one between a captain and his crew. Wherever the captain of a ship goes, everyone is obligated to follow. That can be pretty scary if your captain happens to be the one-legged Ahab character . . . as our friend Ishmael is about to find out.

Chapter Ten

After almost a year at sea, the *Pequod* ventured into the largest ocean in the world, the Pacific. Sailing northward, we began to pass the islands of Formosa and the Philippines. Ahab's zigzagging course was carrying us through most every known sperm whale ground in the world. Long ago, we stopped seeing the mysterious silver-white spout, but the men still kept a sharp lookout for any possible sign of Moby Dick.

The Pacific is the calmest of oceans. Its blue waters roll even and peaceful, reflecting the rays of a powerful sun. Even though it was winter again, the weather was warm enough for us to walk the decks shirtless.

Captain Ahab, however, was anything *but* calm. He charted and recharted the ship's course. His eyes smoldered like coals, and his beard grew as gnarled as tree roots. He seldom slept, but when he did, nightmare screams came forth from his cabin. Not trusting the men to keep a sharp enough watch, Ahab had a contraption built, by which he could be hoisted atop the mainmast by pulley and rope. Finding Moby Dick, I realized, was an obsession with Captain Ahab.

I guess we all get obsessed about something now and then. We get a single idea stuck in our head and we can't think of anything else. Truth be told, I frequently get that way about food.

One morning I sat upon the deck, cleaning my ears with my special paw-scratching method. I saw Ahab approach the blacksmith and say, "I want ye to forge me a special harpoon—something that will stick in Moby Dick like his own fin bone. Use twelve iron rods twined together for the shank, and here's what ye'll use for the barb."

Ahab tossed a leather pouch on the deck. The blacksmith opened the pouch and said admiringly, "Ah, well, razors made of the finest steel."

"Quick, forge me the harpoon!" Ahab demanded.

Soon the blacksmith was sweating away by the flame of his portable forge. He melted the steel, shaped it, banged it with a hammer at his iron anvil. Ahab watched every move with a crazed expression. Behind him I saw the gold doubloon nailed to the mainmast, glinting fiercely in the firelight.

Turning my muzzle, I noticed Ahab's private harpooner standing nearby. He seemed to utter a prayer. The man's name was Fedallah, and with the possible exception of Ahab, he was the most puzzling fellow on the ship. He never spoke a word to anyone except Ahab and his stowaway mates. I could never figure out the man's age or country of origin, because he always wore a wide-brimmed hat that darkened his face with shadow. Perhaps oddest of all, the man gave off practically no scent.

Nearby, Stubb, the second mate, and Flask, the third mate, also watched. "Mr. Stubb, I don't like that harpooner chap," Flask remarked matter-of-factly. "I think he's placed a magic spell on the captain somehow. Ahab used to be a good, honest Quaker man. But I understand he now practices some bizarre foreign religion. Perhaps this harpooner's a priest of that sect."

"Or perhaps he's the Prince of Darkness," Stubb said, less merry than usual. "The Devil in disguise. That hat of his might be hiding both face and horns. Aye, perhaps Ahab signed over his soul, provided the Devil will help him snag this Moby Dick. Which means we've all signed on to the bargain. It's against *my* religion to get angry at anybody, Mr. Flask, but I don't like this harpooner chap, either."

When the blacksmith plunged the newly forged harpoon into a tub of water, it sent up a threatening hiss.

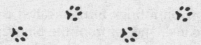

Soon we killed another sperm whale, which brought our total to seven. It was always hard work catching a whale, but it was ever harder work processing the whale afterward.

First the upper half of the whale's head was cut off and lifted by hook alongside the ship. Then the three harpooners went to work on it.

"Down he go!" Tashtego yelled as he and Queequeg lowered Dagoo by rope to the top of the partial head. Dagoo made a slice, then dipped in a pole with a bucket attached to the end of it. When Dagoo pulled the bucket up, it was filled with an oily substance called spermaceti.

As bucket after bucket followed, the spermaceti was poured into huge casks, or barrels. When a cask was full, a group of men would put a top on it, then roll it down to a very big chamber low in the ship known as the hold. For some reason, this particular work reminded me of the way a dog buried his bones.

"Careful, boys," advised Starbuck, the chief mate, as he watched. "Try not to spill a single drop!"

This was partly a joke, as the average sperm whale produces around five hundred gallons of spermaceti. Nevertheless, it is the stuff from which the best and most expensive candles in the world are made.

As the spermaceti was being removed, the rest of us worked at stripping the whale's body of its blubber, which is a layer of thick fat right beneath the skin. It was a little like peeling the rind off an orange, only a thousand times more difficult. This task done, we cut the blubber into smaller pieces, which we tossed into huge iron pots.

"Light the furnace!" Flask called. The pots sat near

the ship's bow on a brick furnace called the try-works. Soon a fire roared, and oil from the blubber bubbled to the surface.

I was one of the men whose job it was to scoop out the oil with ladles and toss it into a cooling tank. After cooling, the oil was poured by several other men into more big casks, which were also stored in the hold.

The oil from a sperm whale's blubber was the best thing you could buy for lighting a lamp or lantern. I knew my paws would be busy ladling a long while because the average sperm whale produces about ten tons or twenty thousand pounds of it!

By then the deck was a bustling factory, overrun with fire smoke, oil, blood, blubber, and heavily sweating men. I gave a shake of my muzzle. My black nose was having a rough time of it. All sorts of smells were coming at me, and most of them were the opposite of pleasant.

"Cheer up," Stubb said, seeing my discomfort. "Whale steak tonight!"

"Yech!" I replied. I'm the least picky eater in the world, but whale meat turned out to taste no better than rubber. Stubb was the only one of us who had a liking for it.

We worked through the night. Light was no problem, though, considering how much oil we now carried aboard. Lanterns dangled all across the ship's rigging, radiating brightness like miniature suns.

Once, through a fog of black smoke, I saw Ahab watching me ladle out the endless oil with my tired paws. I'm sure he cared nothing for this particular whale or the profits it would bring. He was probably just wondering if someone should have asked the creature where Moby Dick was before we slaughtered it.

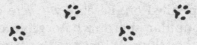

Myself, I stopped caring if we found Moby Dick or not. Something else occupied my mind. After crawling around the damp hold for many hours, searching for a leaky cask, Queequeg fell seriously ill.

He kept to his bunk, overcome with fever. His tattooed body lost much weight, and even his face seemed a paler shade of purplish-yellow. There was no doctor aboard, so I spent much time by his side, doing what little I could to help.

At one point, Queequeg turned his sweat-drenched head to me and said, "My friend, Ishmael, I going to die."

"No," I protested.

"Yes," he said, his noble eyes still glowing. "I can feel it happening. Look-ee, I do not want to be sewn in cloth and tossed in sea. I want proper coffin. On my island, dead people are put in coffin-canoe. Then coffin-canoe is placed on water. This way, dead person can float to shining isle of star in sky. I want carpenter to build me such a coffin. You ask-ee him. And make sure coffin sealed up so no leak."

I felt my ears and tail drooping. "We'll discuss this another time," I said, hoping against hope that the coffin wouldn't be necessary. "For now, let's just see about getting you well."

"I go sleep-ee now," Queequeg said quietly.

He closed his eyes. As my friend slept, I lay on the floor and buried my head in my paws. I didn't want anyone to see or hear that I was whimpering with sadness.

The ship sailed on. Because we were now cruising through a popular sperm whale ground, we met a number of other ships. Whenever this happened, Ahab would call through a speaking-horn, "Has thou seen the White Whale?"

If the answer was yes, Ahab would pay a quick visit to the neighboring ship. Though several men had seen Moby Dick in the past, none had done so on their current voyage. The captain of an English whaling vessel had actually lost an arm to Moby Dick a year before. He now sported a whalebone replacement very similar to Ahab's false leg.

Then we met a ship that had encountered Moby Dick quite recently. It was an American ship named the *Rachel*. "Hast thou seen the White Whale?" Ahab called through his horn as the vessel approached.

"Aye!" the *Rachel*'s captain called back. "Please allow me to board your ship!"

The request granted, the *Rachel*'s captain rowed over and climbed aboard the *Pequod*'s deck. His name was Gardiner, and he was an acquaintance of Ahab's from Nantucket. Much like Ahab, he was unshaven and wore a tormented look.

"When did'st thou see him?" Ahab demanded after a quick greeting.

I lifted my ears a bit to better hear the answer.

"Yesterday," Gardiner said with distress. "We saw his spout, followed, then glimpsed his white hump and head. Our boats gave chase. One of them managed to harpoon the whale, but the whale ran like a gale northeast, dragging the boat out of view. I'm sure the men cut themselves loose from the whale at some point, but the boat never returned. Since last night we've been searching, every man on the lookout, but still . . . nothing."

"Yesterday," Ahab said, sparks seeming to fly from his eyes.

"I need you to help me locate the lost boat," Gardiner told Ahab. "I'll pay you for the time. I'll pay generously."

"Two ships searching for one rowboat," Stubb said with a chuckle. "Why so anxious, Captain? Did one of those lost men happen to be borrowing your silver watch?"

Captain Gardiner grimaced with pain. "Nay, sir. My son is aboard that boat. My twelve-year-old boy. I was teaching him the whaling trade, same way my own father taught me. He was eager to learn, bless the boy. Now I fear he's learning the trade from the meanest of schoolmasters. Captain Ahab, I beg of you, as a fellow man from the sand of Nantucket, please, please, help me find my boy!"

"Ah, Lord have mercy," Flask murmured.

I felt that itch I sometimes get when something disturbs me a great deal. I scratched it with one of my back paws.

Starbuck, always the decent one, stepped forward. "Captain, we must help this man. Certainly you see that. We simply must!" Every man on deck appealed to Ahab with their eyes, willing him to agree to the desperate request of Captain Gardiner.

"We have no time," Ahab whispered intensely. "The White Whale is not far, and we must find him."

"Captain Ahab," Gardiner said, grabbing Ahab's arm, "I beg of you to help! For God's sake, sir, my boy is only twelve years old!"

Ahab pulled away from the man. "Sir, I must bid you farewell. At once!"

I scratched the itch again.

Captain Gardiner fell to his knees pleading, yet Ahab stood there unmoving. Eventually a tearful Captain Gardiner left the ship. Soon we saw the sails of the *Rachel* disappearing on the horizon.

By that time Ahab was standing near the helm with his quadrant, a brass device used for gauging direction based on the sun's position. I watched as Ahab looked through the eyepiece, then quickly calculated figures with a pencil on the whalebone of his leg.

Suddenly Ahab flung the pencil away and screamed a terrible curse, as if he had been bashed across the face by a hammer. Every eye on deck swung around to look at him. I felt my tail creep between my legs.

Ahab craned his face to the fiery noonday sun and cried out, "Sun, thou tellest me faithfully where I am, but thou can'st not tell me where the blasted White Whale be! Why? Why? Why? I ask. Thou seest him this very moment, yet sayest nothing! Very well! I shall find the whale by my own sharp wits! And this quadrant, this toy, this plaything made by man, is equally useless!"

With a furious gesture, Ahab smashed the quadrant onto the deck, instantly breaking it apart. All of us, officers and crew, watched in shock.

My blood ran cold. There is no king on earth with more authority over his people than the captain of a ship far out at sea. The men are at the complete mercy of his will. And, in that moment, I realized that our king, our captain, the leader of our pack, was totally out of his mind!

Chapter Eleven

The *Pequod* hurried madly toward the coast of Japan, then spun around and dove south again. Two-thirds of the earth's surface is covered with water, and I realized we were seeing a sizable portion of it on this voyage. The sun blazed down on us like a ball of flame, scorching my fur. The men went about their work with less enthusiasm now. They grew gloomy, weary, fearful. Ahab spent most daylight hours high atop the mainmast on his pulleyed contraption. His bloodshot eyes were watching, forever watching for Moby Dick.

Queequeg's illness continued, and he finally convinced me to have the coffin built. I was on the deck one morning, helping the carpenter put the finishing touches on it. The day was sweltering-hot, and my pink tongue panted as I worked. As the carpenter sealed up the seams with tar, I noticed a nail sticking out.

"Have you seen the hammer?" I asked the carpenter.

"I thought I left it by the barrel," the carpenter said, pointing.

"I don't see it," I said, squinting through the sun's glare.

"Well, it must be around somewhere," the carpenter replied.

"Here," a voice behind me spoke. A hand offered me the hammer. To my amazement, I saw that the hand belonged to Queequeg! Only a few hours ago he had been at death's door. Now he stood on the sunny deck looking thin but miraculously revived. My tail jumped up and began wagging uncontrollably.

"Queequeg!" I exclaimed. "You seem . . . better! You're on your feet, and your face looks to be a very healthy shade of purple and yellow! What happened, friend?"

Queequeg gave a simple shrug. "I remember I owe money to man back in America. I need to pay. So I get better-ee."

"Just like that?" I asked with great surprise.

"If man decide not to die," Queequeg said calmly, "he do not have to die. All depend on how you look-ee at things. When I use wheelbarrow first time, I pick it up to carry on my shoulder. See, different ways to see different things."

"You sound like the white-haired chaplain, Father Mapple," I said, giving my friend's leg the friendliest of nuzzles. In return, Queequeg showed his dagger-sharp teeth in the friendliest of smiles.

One person wasn't happy about this new development, though.

"Blast it!" the carpenter said, banging the coffin with disgust. "You can't get better, man. If you don't pass away, all the fine work that I have done on this coffin will be for naught!"

"Oh, no," Queequeg said, kneeling down to examine the coffin. "This make very good storage chest. I carve top and make very beautiful."

Queequeg went to work on it right away, and he made that coffin very beautiful, indeed.

A few days later, it seemed we might all need coffins. In these most peaceful of all waters hid the deadliest of all storms—the typhoon. It burst upon us one dark night like an exploding bomb. I didn't even smell it coming.

Thunder boomed, lightning flashed, and rain slashed its way through a howling wind. Monstrous waves tossed the *Pequod* with such force that men staggered and slid dangerously back and forth across the decks. You could hear every rope and piece of wood on the ship strain against the storm's fury. My fur was so drenched with water that my weight seemed to double.

As the Manxman steered the big wheel, I tied him to it with a rope to keep him upright. A wave pounded the ship, and the compass needle spun in a crazy circle. "This storm's a bad sign!" the elderly Manxman shouted over the wind. "Be it God, the forces of Nature, or whatever, it's warning us to turn away!"

"Look out!" the Dutchman cried, as a giant wave ripped one of the spare rowboats from the starboard gunwale. Down on the main deck, I saw Stubb, Flask, and some other men frantically tying the other rowboats tighter in place. Stubb sang loudly as he labored:

> *"Oh, jolly is the gale,*
> *And a joker is the whale,*
> *A-flourishin' his tail—"*

"Come on, and join me, Mr. Flask," Stubb called. "It'll keep up your spirits!"

"I'm not much for singing, Mr. Stubb," Flask called back.

Starbuck charged over to them, yelling, "Listen to me! I can't waken the captain, but we have to change our course. Help me organize the men for the job!"

I made my way down to the main deck, careful to keep my paws from slipping on the wet surface. The officers gathered most of the men, and we began to yank on various ropes to change the angle of the sails. Through sheets of rain, I saw Ahab rise out of a hatch on the upper deck. His face was grim, his gray hair blowing wildly about his head.

A streak of lightning lit the sky, leaving us a ghastly souvenir. The tops of all three masts now glowed with an unearthly bluish-green haze. This event is known as Saint Elmo's Fire, and it happens sometimes to ships at sea during an electrical storm. Still pulling rope, we all stared at the three masts, hypnotized. They burned like three oversized spermaceti candles.

"Lord have mercy on us!" the Manxman exclaimed.

Ahab gazed up at the phosphorescent burning. Out of nowhere, Fedallah appeared and handed him his specially made harpoon.

Then Ahab held the harpoon up to the raging sky and roared, "Very well, ye wish to challenge me! But I am a train rushing across the iron rails of a track! I shan't be swerved one inch from my course!"

The bluish-green glowing leaped higher.

"What's that ye say?" Ahab cried. "I am no match for ye? Ha! No matter what thou throw at me, I accept yer challenge!"

Lightning struck so close it blinded me. I briefly felt the heat on my muzzle. When the lightning left, I saw flames wriggling like serpents at the tip of Ahab's harpoon.

Ahab laughed uproariously at the sight. The fire lit up the long white scar on his face, and I now had a better idea how he got it. Playing with lightning!

"Avast!" Ahab called down to the main deck. "Stop interfering with those sails, or I'll brand ye with my hot harpoon!"

We all stopped hauling at the ropes. Just then, an enormous wave hammered the ship sideways, hurling a flood of water across the deck. I dug my nails into the deck to keep from being swept away.

"Captain," Starbuck yelled over the elements, "if we don't reverse, the storm'll destroy us!"

"Avast, I say!" Ahab screamed back, waving his flaming harpoon at the men. "Leave the sails be! Through the storm we plunge! We follow my course to find Moby Dick with no changes! The day I nailed the doubloon to the mast, every man of ye took an oath to hunt the monster! We drank on it! And, by thunder, we shall hunt the White Whale until he spouts black blood!"

My tail quivered, and I actually smelled the panic that was coming off several of the men around me. They and I realized this lunatic was every bit as terrifying as the typhoon.

"Men, I see thou art afraid!" Ahab shouted louder than the wind. "Fear is a crate of cargo that we have no use for! Watch me, listen to me, follow me! And I, Ahab, thy commander, shall blow out thy fear!"

Ahab brought the harpoon's fiery barb near his face and unleashed a powerful breath. Amazingly, the flame went out.

Crazed as he was, there was something greatly heroic about this man. As I did on the night when I had lapped up the grog, I now felt myself irresistibly pulled toward Captain Ahab's magnetic power.

The ship dared to make its way through the storm

and survived. By the following morning, the typhoon had blown past, leaving the Pacific calmer than ever. The men quietly set about repairing the damaged *Pequod*. Ahab stuck his face into the salted air and sniffed. I was very impressed that he might actually be able to pick up Moby Dick's scent in this manner. Then Ahab ordered the sails set for a southeasterly course.

Finally, the *Pequod* reached the equator. There we sailed through the deepest and most isolated part of the Pacific. We saw no other ships, and knew there was not a speck of land for more than a thousand miles in every direction.

It was in those lonely waters that Moby Dick devoured Captain Ahab's leg. *How fitting,* I thought, *if this turned out to be where we finally found the White Whale.* Somehow, against all reason, every man sensed this was destined to happen.

One cloudless afternoon, I stood on the quarterdeck, practicing my digging technique. The wood didn't work as well as soil, but it was all I had to work with. Taking a rare break from his overhead perch, Ahab stood thoughtfully at the gunwale nearby. I saw Starbuck, the chief mate, approach him. Curious to hear their conversation, I crept closer and hid behind a barrel. I lifted my ears to catch the conversation.

"Mr. Starbuck," Ahab said with a nod of greeting.

"Captain Ahab," Starbuck said, nodding back.

"It's a mild, mild wind and a mild sky," Ahab said, gazing out at the smooth surface of the sea. "On such a day as this, I struck my very first whale. That was, what . . . forty years ago."

"Is that right, sir?"

I could see there was more going on between these two men than just the words they spoke. Starbuck seemed more anxious than usual, and Ahab seemed more willing to speak of himself.

"I've spent most of my life on a ship, and a lonely life it's been," Ahab said, his voice weighted with weariness. "You know, several years ago I finally took a wife, a fair and youthful woman. When I proposed, I suppose I harbored thoughts of settling down. But, no, I sailed off on a three-year voyage the day after my wedding."

Ahab chuckled, and Starbuck smiled tightly.

The captain continued. "I don't know why I myself— or any other man, for that matter—am drawn to the brutal life of a ship at sea. There must be something. Perhaps we believe, somewhere in the water's bottomless depths, we'll glimpse the truth about who we are and what everything is meant for."

I found myself nodding my head with a feeling of understanding.

"I have a wife myself," Starbuck mentioned. "Mary's her name. A small son, as well. Every day Mary carries my boy to the top of the hill so he'll catch the first sight of his father's returning sails."

Ahab turned to Starbuck, showing a look of fondness. "You're a decent fellow, Mr. Starbuck. Listen to me, son. When we finally chase the White Whale, I want ye and yer boat crew to stay on the ship. I don't want ye involved in the chase. Do ye hear? I very much want that wife and child of yours to see ye again."

Starbuck clutched at the gunwale and finally spoke his real feelings. "Oh, Captain, why should any of us tangle with that angry whale? Even if I survive, others may die. I beg you, let us turn the sails this very day and sail homeward."

I raised my ears a bit higher.

Ahab spoke in a hollow tone. "My course is set. It is not within my power to turn back. I'm sorry, but sometimes I think I'm not a captain at all, but only fate's lieutenant. A man following orders that were shouted out a million years ago."

"No, sir," Starbuck said, raising his voice in frustration. "The orders were given the day that whale tore off your leg. Ever since, you've narrowed your vision to only this senseless revenge. Indeed, you seem to pile all the rage and hate of the human race upon the hump of that simple brute! A whale that doesn't even know the *meaning* of the word *evil!*"

Ahab stared at the water.

"Have you lost all feeling for your fellow man?" Starbuck pressed on. "It's bad enough you refused to help Captain Gardiner, but far worse it'll be if you send your own men to their death! Dare you be responsible for such a tragedy? I lost my own father and brother from whaling trips, and I don't wish to lose anyone else I care about! Captain, I beg of you, let us abandon this wild quest!"

Ahab turned to Starbuck, his eyes frozen. "I will not change my mind, Mr. Starbuck. If I triumph, this monstrous White Whale will no longer terrorize the world. If I fail . . . No matter, I will never change from this course!"

Starbuck glared at the captain, then marched off. Ahab returned his eyes to the sea. I turned my head to watch Starbuck.

After a few steps, Starbuck stopped, glanced around, then reached to the back of his pants and pulled out a pistol. I realized he had stolen it from Ahab's cabin, the only place on board where firearms were kept. As the ship gently rocked, Starbuck stared at the pistol, as if wrestling with a difficult decision.

I knew what it was. He was considering either firing upon Captain Ahab, or imprisoning him in his cabin. This done, he would seize command of the *Pequod* and guide us all safely back to Massachusetts.

Unbelievable as it may seem, I wasn't sure I wanted this to happen. Since Queequeg's recovery, my own thoughts had drifted back to Moby Dick. Perhaps, I reasoned, the creature really *was* as evil as Ahab claimed. After all, he had destroyed one man's arm, another man's leg, and he had torn a helpless child from his father. Perhaps he really *was* a demon of the sea that needed to be killed. Or perhaps he wasn't. At any rate, some feeling deep in my belly was urging me, dragging me, forcing me, to see this famous White Whale for myself.

Perhaps Starbuck felt the same way, or perhaps he just felt himself to be no match for the mighty Ahab. The chief mate returned the pistol to his pants and walked solemnly away.

Ahab continued to stare at the endless blue world of waves. I took a few padded steps closer. He spoke to himself, very softly, "Aye, it is a mild, mild wind."

I thought I saw a tear drip from Ahab's eye into the water. If so, it may have become the most precious drop in all the world's oceans, seas, rivers, lakes, and ponds. For that single tear may have been the last remainder of Captain Ahab's humanity.

Several days later, all of our lives were changed forever. Ahab mounted his perch at dawn and watched the calm waves through his telescope. In the late afternoon of that fateful day, Ahab sent up a howling cry.

"There she blows! There she blows! A whale with a hump like a snow hill! It is Moby Dick!"

Okay, mates, this is it. The moment we've all been waiting for. But first . . . Joe and I are also about to make a big sighting!

Chapter Twelve

"It's Richard Everson!" Joe whispered.

Wishbone and Joe were standing alongside a concrete basketball court in Jackson Park. The hefty high-school boy was alone on the court, casually dribbling the basketball. Wishbone could see the "J" marked in black ink, indicating it was the ball given to Joe by his father. There was no one else around, and Everson didn't seem to notice the boy and dog watching him.

"Yep, it's him, all right," Wishbone told Joe. "Same 'White Whale' jacket, same bulldog face, same body big enough to destroy us both without breaking a sweat. Well, mission accomplished, Joe. We ought to go now. Hey, you know what? I think I hear Ellen calling us for an early dinner!"

Everson dribbled the ball downcourt, moving with the grace of a ballet dancer. He spun around once, as if avoiding an opponent, then two strides later hooked the ball over his head for a basket. It was a perfectly executed play.

"Wow! He's really good," Wishbone commented. "Even though we don't like him."

Joe kept his eyes fixed on Everson. "What do I do

now?" he said to himself. "Walk away, or throw caution to the wind?"

"I vote that we keep a firm grip on that caution and walk away," Wishbone advised. "And, remember, a dog's vote always counts double."

Joe didn't budge. He and Wishbone just watched as Everson dribbled the basketball back toward mid-court. When Everson turned to face the basket, he dribbled in place, seeming to focus all his energy on the metal rim and dangling net that lay ahead. Suddenly he charged downcourt fast and ferocious as a speeding cannonball. He shot into the air for a layup and pounded the ball so hard against the backboard it vibrated with noise. The ball fell through the net for a score.

"That is one mean basketball player," Joe said under his breath.

"I agree, he is mean," Wishbone said. "But, you see, I'm worried that his meanness might be making you just a little bit mean yourself. You know what I mean?"

Apparently Joe didn't. A glare smoldered in his eyes as he watched Everson retrieve the ball. Seeming very satisfied with his layup, Everson began to spin the ball on his index finger. Joe's face flushed angrily as the "J" turned into a whirling blur.

"Easy, boy," Wishbone whispered.

Without warning, Joe made a mad dash straight for the ball. With a look of surprise, Everson whipped around to see Joe coming his way. Just before Joe was able to seize the ball, Everson dribbled away with a quick spin.

Joe waited, figuring his next move. Everson's dribbling relaxed into a slow and easy movement. He brushed the blond hair off his forehead. Though his face showed no expression, it seemed the guy was inviting Joe to come and cover him.

Taking the challenge, Joe went into his defensive basketball stance. The boys studied each other, both ready to react. It looked as if they were right in the middle of a hotly contested game.

"Go, Joe!" Wishbone called out. "I'd like to help you, but basketball isn't really my best sport. I'm afraid my legs are a little short."

As Joe followed, Everson dribbled to the left. Joe took a wild swipe at the ball, attempting a steal, but then Everson swung the ball out of reach. Not only was Joe outmatched, Wishbone realized, but he was too upset to be playing his best.

Joe made a desperate lunge for the ball, almost losing his balance. Without missing a beat, Everson dribbled the ball around his back to keep it away.

Frustrated, Joe wiped sweat off his forehead. Everson dribbled the ball a good distance out from the basket, then stopped. He lifted the ball to chest level, preparing to shoot. Joe didn't follow. Instead, he stole a glance back at the basket, and Wishbone knew what he was thinking. If Everson took a shot from this distance, Joe could certainly be the first to fetch the ball.

Everson gave an easy bend to his knees, then sent the ball arching high through the air. The ball swished through the net, barely making a sound.

By the time the ball hit the ground, Joe was right there. In a single swift move, he scooped up the ball and tucked it under his arm.

"Way to go, Joe!" Wishbone called from the sideline. "We got the ball! Now what do you say we high-tail it home?"

Wishbone started to run, but then he saw Joe wasn't leaving the court. Joe stood near the basket, keeping his eyes locked on Everson. A slight smile crossed Everson's lips. The smile puzzled Wishbone, especially because he thought there might be a tiny bit of admiration mixed into it.

Joe didn't smile back, though. Instead, there was a look of fierce determination in his eyes that caused Wishbone deep concern. Slowly, Joe began to walk toward Everson. Wishbone realized Joe wasn't leaving until he had given the last growl on the subject. Wishbone wasn't sure if Joe was being brave or foolish, or a little bit of both. A few feet away from the guy, Joe stopped.

"You know," Joe told his opponent, "it's not hard to see why you got kicked off the Wilson team."

"Hey, don't make him angry," Wishbone urged. "Uh . . . well . . . I think it's too late."

Everson was staring angrily, just as he had right before he first made off with the ball.

Wishbone was watching carefully, ready to help his master the second he was needed.

With lightning speed, Everson leaped at Joe, snatched the ball from his hands, and streaked away from the court. Joe stood there, watching, almost stunned. Everson looked back once over his shoulder, then continued on his way. Soon he crossed a wooden footbridge that led over a stream deeper into the park.

"What do we do now?" Wishbone called out to Joe.

"All right," Joe said to himself. "If he wants a chase, I'll give him the chase of his life!"

"So be it," Wishbone declared. "If we go down, by gosh, we're going down together!"

Joe and Wishbone dashed away, soon bounding over the footbridge in pursuit of Richard Everson.

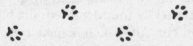

Oh, boy, here we go! On the way through the park, though, let's take a slight detour to the Pacific Ocean. Don't forget, Ishmael and the men are just about to get their first look at you-know-who.

Chapter Thirteen

"There she blows!" Ahab cried again. "Moby Dick! There! There! By thunder, there she blows!"

The moment Ahab first called out Moby Dick's name, all of us scrambled up into the rigging to have a look at the legendary whale. Hanging from a rope with my teeth and front paws, I scanned the blue water. Sure enough, about a mile in the distance, I caught sight of a gleaming white hump rising and falling with the sea's gentle swell. There came an upward gush of silvery whiteness. It seemed to be the very same spout we had chased several months before in the Indian Ocean.

"We give chase!" Ahab shouted triumphantly. "Put the sails on course! Turn the wheel! Mr. Starbuck, stay aboard the ship! Lower the boats!"

In a rush of frenzied action, all the captain's orders were carried out. The ship chased the whale, but I was too busy helping with the lowering of my boat to watch. As you may recall, Ahab forbade Starbuck and his crew from taking part in the chase against Moby Dick. Normally this would have kept me out of the chase. But one of Ahab's boatmen had injured his hand, so I, perhaps foolishly, had volunteered to take his place. I had traveled too many miles to miss this moment.

The sea was remarkably smooth, and the boats glided through it as if they were three hollowed-out shells. Facing us from the stern, Ahab stared ahead, his eyes as sharp as his harpoon's steel barb. As I rowed, I gave a nod at Queequeg, who had joined the crew of Flask's boat.

I don't know if Moby Dick sensed us or not, but, from a twitch in Ahab's face, I knew we were fairly close. I swerved around my muzzle as I rowed. Not far away, the upper portion of Moby Dick's head and hump sparkled white as freshly fallen snow in the bright sunlight. I could tell he was even more gigantic than the other whales we had seen. Yet, despite his size, the water rippled playfully around him. The ease and speed and joyfulness with which this whale swam filled me with a sense of wonder.

Suddenly the great hump arched upward, revealing several twisted black objects, which I realized were harpoons permanently lodged in him. The immense whale briefly displayed its tail flukes. Then the creature slanted downward, diving beneath the waves. For now, Moby Dick had gone out of sight.

Ahab raised a hand. Oars came up, and the three boats driftd. Fedallah, Ahab's harpooner, stood up in the bow of our boat, motionless as a statue. Everyone glanced over the surrounding sea, wondering if Moby Dick was done spouting, or if he would soon reappear.

We waited . . . and waited . . . and waited . . .

To refresh myself, I dipped a paw in the calm water. Through the blueness I noticed a small circle of white, no bigger than a dinner plate. As I wondered what it was, it floated slowly upward, magnifying in size. My heart jumped in my throat when I realized it was Moby Dick's giant head. I gaped at the long body and, beneath it, a jaw that looked strangely crooked.

"It's him!" Ahab gasped. "Turn the boat!" As we frantically backpaddled to get the boat facing the whale, Ahab and Fedallah both snatched up their harpoons, at the ready. But by the time we were in position, the whale had disappeared.

I wondered if this was luck, or if the whale really did have a degree of intelligence. Then I whipped around to see the massive head lifting through the water on the other side of our boat. The monstrous jaw yawned open, revealing a row of sharp triangular teeth, each one big enough to kill a man. The whale was lying on its side so it could fully use the mouth that lay on the underside of its head.

All hands rushed to the stern. Water spurted through the air, drenching my fur, and all our bodies were jolted up and down. The whale was chomping the wooden boat clean in half as if his teeth were a pair of oversized shears.

Everyone was tossed overboard. I treaded the wild waves created by the great beast's thrashings, as did the rest of the crew. By now, Moby Dick was swimming in a wide circle around us, his body creating a circle of frothy whiteness. We all screamed for the other two boats to rescue us, but they hesitated, fearful of crossing Moby Dick's path.

Struggling to keep his head above water, Ahab yelled at the top of his lungs, "Mr. Starbuck! Sail our way! It'll drive the whale off!"

The *Pequod,* which had been nearby, aimed straight toward us, soon cutting through the deadly circle. With relief, I saw Moby Dick's awesome white shape shooting away underwater.

We all scrambled aboard the *Pequod,* eager to escape the threatening whale. I gave myself a good shake to get rid of some of the water that covered me. As several men hauled Ahab on deck, I saw that the old man still clung to his treasured harpoon.

Stumbling to the gunwale, Ahab called to the other two boats. "Mr. Stubb, Mr. Flask. Don't stand there gawking! Get after him. We'll have another boat down in a flash!"

Fortunately, no one was seriously hurt in our first chase of the mighty White Whale. We spent the rest of the day searching the ocean. But Moby Dick seemed to have vanished. When sunset finally bled through the sky, all hands were brought aboard and Ahab called us together.

"We'll keep the mainmast manned all through the night," the captain said, his eyes blazing like flame. "Sing out the second ye see his spout. Take heed, though, he could be traveling in any direction. He's a murderous monster, but there's a great intelligence about him."

Based on what I'd seen that day, I realized Ahab might have been right about his remark.

Ahab pointed to the gold doubloon nailed to the mainmast. "I spotted the White Whale first, and so I earned this coin myself. But I'm a fair-minded man. I'll give ye men another chance. Whosoever spots Moby Dick on the day he's killed, ye shall have this coin. And if I'm the one who sees him that day, ten times the coin's value shall be divided among ye!"

"Huzza! Huzza! Huzza!" the rest of the men and I shouted. Why did we cheer this most dangerous of chases? It is difficult to answer this. I think perhaps on the night Captain Ahab guided us through the typhoon, he somehow made us feel that we were indestructible.

Though exhausted, all of us were too excited to sleep much. And I'm sure Ahab never once shut his eyes.

At daybreak the three mastheads were taken over by fresh crew members, and the ship glided swiftly with the wind. The only chore any of us did that morning was watch the water—from the masts, gunwales, ropes, every possible position. Yet for hours all we saw was the blue and very calm Pacific.

Then all of us beheld him at once.

First we heard a distant surge of water. Then Moby Dick burst through the sea and leaped unbelievably high into the air. He was perhaps only half a mile away. The complete form of his colossal bulk seemed to remain momentarily in midair, as if by magic. Around his whiteness, a spray glittered in the sun like a glacier. Then, leading with his head, he dove downward, landing with a splash so shattering that it might have been felt all the way to China.

This wondrous airborne leap is known as "breaching," and no one knows why the whale does it. A person could sail the world every day of his or her life and never see a sight half so breathtaking.

"Ye defy us with thy breach!" Ahab shouted at the whale. "And for that I admire ye. But, Moby Dick, thy hour and my harpoon are at hand! Men, lower the boats!"

We cranked down the boats, dropped into them, and rowed forcefully away from the ship. Most any other whale in the world would have tried to flee from us. But not Moby Dick.

As Ahab steered from the stern, I saw his eyes jump wide open with alarm. Instinctively, my tail jumped, too. "He's turned around!" Ahab yelled loud enough for the men in all three boats to hear. "He's making straight for the boats! Very well, then, we'll take him forehead to forehead! When we're close, we'll be out of the sideways vision of his eyes. A perfect chance to throw! All three boats, make straight for the whale!"

We rowed for all we were worth.

"Stroke, men, stroke!" Ahab commanded. "Break yer backs! Straight for the whale! Nay, don't glance back! I shall guide ye! Stroke, men, stroke!"

As I rowed, I heard a growing roar of water behind me. Unable to resist, I turned my head for a look.

A shiver ran through my fur. Moby Dick was plowing directly at our boat. His enormous blunt forehead was raised partially out of the water, his body spewing out a raging white wake. Though there are virtually no features on a sperm whale's head, I could have sworn Moby Dick had a murderous look on his face.

"Ishmael, face me!" Ahab yelled. "Not the whale!"

Even though I kept on rowing, I couldn't look away. How could I? We were on a collision course with an animal the size of an avalanche! With every stroke, my heart pounded in my chest. Moby Dick's watery roar grew so loud it was deafening. Tall Fedallah stood motionless in the bow, his harpoon held steady, ready to strike. Every second Moby Dick's cruel face loomed larger—LARGER—LARGER!

"Harpooners, strike!" Ahab screamed.

Fedallah, Queequeg, Tashtego, and Dagoo all hurled their harpoons. I'm not sure how many of them struck, or even what happened next. Everything became chaos. Torrents of flying water—wildly thrashing ropes—a flash of flukes—the whale's monstrous head and deformed jaw. All the while, my boat was bouncing on the water as if it were a child's ball.

Soon everything calmed down. My fur still bristled with fear, but the boat and I had remained in one piece.

Then I saw that the other two boats had been splintered to bits. All crew members were in the ocean, struggling and thrashing to stay above the tumbling waves. Fortunately, Moby Dick seemed to have fled the scene.

"Signal the ship!" called Flask, the third mate, as he bobbed. "Someone please signal the ship!"

"Without delay!" called Stubb, the second mate, between spits of salty water. "We're in the soup, and we need someone to ladle us out!"

I found myself chuckling. *It's a funny thing,* I thought. *Though the average whaling man spends most of his life on water, he swims no better than an overweight cat. And everyone knows—*

A low rumble sounded. Right beneath my tail. Something thundered beneath the boat. Next thing I knew, I was shooting straight up as if shot like an arrow. The world spun upside down, blurring sea and sky, as the boat somersaulted through the air.

With a violent crash, I hit the water and shot downward. I fought my way up with all fours, found darkness, realized I was under the overturned boat, then swam away. I broke through the surface, gasping for air.

Oh, what a horrible vision I saw. Nearby, Moby Dick arched upward, and I saw Fedallah lashed to his massive white flank by a tangle of harpoon lines. The man's black eyes stared at me lifelessly, then disappeared beneath the waves.

Done with his murderous business, Moby Dick swam away, dragging the trail of harpoon lines behind him as he went.

Minutes later the *Pequod* picked up its scattered crew members, most of whom had suffered nothing worse than sprains and bruises. As Ahab dragged himself onto the deck, though, I saw that his whalebone leg had been snapped into a sharp splinter. The kindly chief mate, Starbuck, rushed to help the old man up.

"How the bone gores me!" Ahab cried in pain. "No matter. It seems everyone has made it back. Yes, that's good. No, wait . . . where is Fedallah?"

"He's gone, sir," I told Ahab. "Tangled in the lines and dragged under."

Leaning on Starbuck, Ahab released a beastly groan of despair. "Captain, listen to reason," Starbuck pleaded. "Never, never, never will you capture him! He snapped the line of every harpoon that hit him! I tell you, he'll swamp every one of us! It is madness to hunt him more!"

Ahab swung away from Starbuck and grasped at the gunwale. "Avast!" he shouted. "I am madness maddened! But what I've dared I've willed, and what I've willed I'll do! By thunder, I'll kill the whale yet!"

That night hammers pounded and the grindstone hummed as we worked by lantern light repairing the damaged boats. The carpenter also found time to create a new leg for Ahab. We slept less that night than the previous one.

The following day dawned as fair as a summer in paradise. Sea and sky merged in perfect blueness. It was the kind of day that made me thankful to be alive, and I very much hoped I would remain that way.

Yes, the White Whale now filled us all with terror, but we were not ready to surrender. We watched and watched for Moby Dick. Ahab feverishly paced the deck on his new whalebone leg, gazing every which way.

At noon, the captain cried out with fury, "No, blast him, he's outsmarted us. He's behind, chasing us. Not the other way around. I feel it in every one of my creaky bones! Reverse the ship!"

The sails were adjusted, allowing us to cruise against the wind. Ahab had himself lifted to the top of the mainmast. For hours we sailed, every man searching the waves. Suspense hung in every breath of breeze, every creak of the ropes, every nervous tap of my tail on the deck.

Feeling the need to see Queequeg, I found him watching from a gunwale. We stood together in silence for a while. Then Queequeg finally said, "That whale is big-ee."

"Yes, very big-ee," I agreed.

Queequeg smiled at me. "Is it too late for us to change mind and go fish-ee for lobster?"

I chuckled.

He gave my back a quick scratch, and I returned the favor by giving his hand a few affectionate licks.

Ahab's voice pierced the moment. "There she blows!"

The other men on the mastheads echoed with a chorus of "There she blows! There! There! There! She blows! She blows!"

I pulled myself up on the rigging for a better look. A quarter-mile away, Moby Dick's proud spout fountained high in the air. Something hovered above his snowy head like a halo. Shielding out the sun's glare with a paw, I saw that the halo was actually a circle of flying white birds. As the spouting continued, the ship drew closer. Now, around every gush, I saw a multicolored rainbow shimmering in the mist. The beauty of the vision filled my eyes with tears. I wiped away the wetness with one of my front paws.

Ahab landed on the deck and announced, "I've sighted the whale on the day of his death! The day he spouts his last! Therefore, ten times the doubloon's value will be split among every man! Lower the boats!"

I was undecided as to what I should do. True, I was on a whaling expedition and had helped to catch many whales. Yet it suddenly pained me to think of killing this glorious creation.

For the third and final time, the boats were lowered and we chased Moby Dick. He must have been tired from the ongoing war, because we pulled close to him very quickly. Just as Queequeg, Tashtego, and Dagoo were prepared to heave their harpoons, Moby Dick gave a mighty downward slap with his tail. Suddenly, we were all blinded by a flying wall of water.

At Ahab's command, we rowed through it, closing in on the whale, trying to give the harpooners a shot. Then I saw the huge flukes swing through the air, back and forth, back and forth, amazingly fast, bashing all three boats. Water splashed so hard it hurt, and men yelled, and then—Moby Dick was gone.

None of the boats was destroyed, but they had all sprung leaks, the other two being in worse shape than ours. "Mr. Stubb, Mr. Flask," Ahab ordered. "Away to the ship. Repair yer boats—and quickly, at that! We've no more spares!"

Stubb and Flask guided their wounded boats back to the *Pequod.* "Sir," one of the men in our boat spoke. "We're also taking on water. Perhaps we should return to the ship as well."

"Row for the whale!" Ahab roared as he picked up his harpoon. "We must destroy the monster before he destroys us first!"

In the distance, I saw Moby Dick's giant mass gliding away beneath the water. The tired men in my boat rowed after the tired whale. I, however, did not row.

Facing Ahab would take as much courage as facing Moby Dick, but I was determined. "Sir," I told Ahab in a firm voice, "Moby Dick doesn't mean to destroy us. He could have killed every one of us just now, but he didn't. All he seeks is the chance to survive!"

"Silence!" Ahab cried, rising clumsily and making his way for the boat's bow.

I stood up, blocking Ahab's path. "Don't you see?" I said, tilting my head upward at him. "That's why he was swimming in the opposite direction this morning. With all my heart, I believe the White Whale just wants to be free of us! Let us share the sea with him in peace!"

Ahab raised his harpoon, as if to plunge it into my furred chest. "Nay!" he howled like a hurricane. "This whale who stole my leg—forever crippling me, body and soul—is a miserable, wicked, vicious, malicious creature of pure evil!"

"He's evil only to you," I barked, "because you refuse to view him in any other light!"

Ahab closed his eyes in anguish, shutting out anything but his wild obsession. Then he shoved me aside and limped to the boat's bow. We were now close upon the whale. Sensing our position, Moby Dick slapped his flat flukes against the water with awesome force. Water showered around us, the boat bounced backward, and I alone went flying overboard. Upon landing, I treaded the waves with my paws, glancing around fearfully.

"We're half-full of water now!" one of the men called to Ahab. "We won't float much longer!"

"Bring me another boat!" Ahab screamed at the nearby *Pequod*. "By thunder, on this day Moby Dick's tail shall be tied to the ship! Starbuck, Stubb, Flask— anyone—bring me another boat!"

I saw Moby Dick's squarish head rise from the water.

As if he understood Ahab's words, the whale was barreling straight for the ship with all his might. Queequeg, Tashtego, and Dagoo were now mounted atop the three mastheads. Each of them hollered out a warning to their mates below.

Every hair on my body shot up. "No!" I cried out. "Not the ship! Not my beloved friends!"

Timbers split and men fell screaming. Using his tremendous head as a battering ram, Moby Dick had smashed the side of the ship to smithereens. The whale disappeared as a torrent of water flooded through the *Pequod*'s destroyed hull.

Terrified, I dogpaddled my fastest for Ahab's boat. "Come on, lad," Ahab called to me. "Ye see I'm right now! Help me kill this monster at once! Then we shall have plenty enough whalebone to fix the ship!"

Suddenly I stopped.

The upper half of the whale surfaced several yards from the boat. I saw one of the tiny black eyes, and it seemed to be focused directly on Ahab. Very slowly, Ahab turned his scarred face to his foe. The whale lay there, quiet, motionless, a magnificent white mountain in the middle of the sea. For whatever reason, Moby Dick was allowing Ahab to make the next move in the game.

Ahab gave a silent gesture, and his men rowed the leaky boat alongside the whale's glistening flank. With great care, Ahab gripped his harpoon and balanced his dead leg on the bow's rim.

Ahab lifted the harpoon. Instead of throwing the weapon, I could see he was planning to stab Moby Dick to death.

Ahab fixed his fiery eyes on the whale. Moby Dick's tiny black eye seemed to stare right back. My own brown eyes watched the entire scene most intently.

Ahab spoke in a bitter, whispering hiss. "I turn my body from the sun! To the last I grapple with thee, Moby Dick! For hate's sake, I spit my last breath at thee! Thus I give up the spear!"

With all his power, Ahab plunged the harpoon into the whale's snow-white hump. A fountain of dark blood gushed forth, spraying Ahab's face. The whale thrashed his monumental body in spasms of pain, churning up a tormented foam.

Still alive with strength, Moby Dick charged forward. The harpoon's line shot like lightning through its grooves. When the line caught on a spare lance, Ahab stooped to clear it. The captain screamed with agony as the rope instantly seized him around the neck, yanked him off his one leg, and threw him violently overboard. The whale's sudden flight jerked the boat with such force that it toppled over, dashing all crew members into the ocean. As the waves rolled against my face, I struggled to keep my muzzle above water.

Breathlessly, I watched as the men struggled and the whale dragged the strangling captain through the waves. The flukes flew upward and the gigantic white creature made a downward dive. At that, Moby Dick and Captain Ahab disappeared beneath the waves, neither to be seen by me again.

I saw the rowboat sinking into the sea. I turned my head to the *Pequod*. With utter horror, I saw the ship being swallowed in a swirling tornado of water, only the upper part of its masts yet remaining in the air.

Our last hope of being saved was gone!

Whoa! That was intense! I need a break. But I don't get a break, because Joe and I are chasing after Richard Everson. I hope he doesn't turn out to be as dangerous as Moby Dick!

Chapter Fourteen

Joe and Wishbone ran through the park, all six of their legs flying after the fleeing Richard Everson.

"Faster!" Joe cried.

Joe and Wishbone shifted into high gear. Because it was spring, the trees were in full blossom, changing the park into a sea of lush greenery. Scents of nature flooded Wishbone's nose—leaves, dirt, grass, insects, birds, maybe a cat somewhere. But Wishbone kept his eyes glued to Everson, whose dark blue jacket was weaving in and out of view among the plentiful trees ahead.

A thud sounded. "Ow!" Joe screamed. Wishbone whipped around to see that Joe had fallen. The boy gritted his teeth as he clutched at one of his knees.

"You okay?" Wishbone asked with concern.

Joe forced himself to get up off the ground. "I just tripped. Come on, we can't let him get away!"

Joe and Wishbone resumed the chase, even though Joe was now limping a bit. Everson had increased his lead, and soon Wishbone saw the "white whale" emblem disappear through a thick curtain of trees.

When Joe and Wishbone reached the area, they

stopped, both breathing hard. From there it was impossible to see where Everson had disappeared to. Wishbone lowered his nose to the ground and began sniffing here, there, everywhere.

"We lost him again," Joe said, rubbing his wounded knee. "He could have gone west toward the highway, east back toward the center of town, or north toward the pond. If we go the wrong way, he's gone for good. Uh . . . let's go for east."

As Joe hobbled away, Wishbone barked, causing Joe to turn. "No, he went north," Wishbone said, pointing with his nose. "Trust me on this. I'm a dog. I come from a long line of experienced hunters."

"You picked up his scent?" Joe asked.

"Aye, aye, sir."

Wishbone and Joe went through the curtain of trees, their feet crunching over fallen twigs. Soon they broke through to an open expanse of grass. On the far side of the area was a duck pond and a few empty benches. Several duck families glided peacefully across the water's glassy surface.

"There he runs!" Wishbone called, catching sight of the "white whale" emblem. Everson was on the other side of the pond, just about to escape through a cluster of trees at the park's northern boundary.

"Hey, Everson!" Joe called out at full volume.

Everson stopped and turned, still holding the basketball.

"Let me tell you something!" Joe shouted.

Wishbone heard not only anger in Joe's voice, but also pain. Wishbone knew why. Joe treasured anything that reminded him of his father, whom he deeply missed.

"You're not just a menace on the basketball court!" Joe hollered. "You're a menace to the entire town of

Oakdale! I'm telling you for the last time, I want my ball back!"

Wishbone threw out his most ferocious bark in support.

Even from that distance, Wishbone's sharp eyes could see an expression of rage cross Everson's face. His lips twisted, his eyes bugged open, and he generally looked as if he was about to explode. Wishbone feared Everson was about to run over and do him and Joe some serious physical damage.

Instead, Everson heaved back his arm and hurled the basketball with tremendous force. The worn orange ball sailed through the air, then—*ker-plash!*—landed smack in the middle of the duck pond.

Circles of water rippled outward from the ball to the edges of the pond. The ducks hurried away with a flurry of frightened quacks.

Wishbone saw his chance to save the day. He galloped for the pond, calling, "Don't worry, Joe. 'Fetch the ball' is one of my best activities! I'll fish that thing out of the water faster than you can say 'Feed the dog!' "

"Wishbone, what are you doing?" Joe called.

"Just watch!"

All four feet left the ground and Wishbone went flying heroically through the air. With a splash, the cool water rushed up around the dog's fur. Without a moment's pause, Wishbone dogpaddled straight for the basketball, which sat motionless in the middle of the pond.

Most of the ducks were well out of the way, but one of the bigger ones swam right into the dog's path. "Hey, Moby Duck," Wishbone called, "you wanna get out of my way? I'm chasing a ball here!"

The duck quacked loudly, as if honking a car's horn at a busy intersection. Wishbone answered with a loud

growl that sent the duck fluttering upward. A few more quick strokes and Wishbone was right beside the ball.

"Wishbone, come back here!" Joe yelled from the shore.

"Just give me a sec," Wishbone answered. "You want your ball back, don't . . . Uh-oh."

Wishbone discovered a problem. The basketball was twenty times bigger than the balls with which he usually played fetch. There was no way he would be able to get his mouth around it. *This is one of those times when hands would be very useful,* Wishbone thought as he studied the ball. *Fortunately, I've got a brilliant mind and . . . yes, I see another solution!*

Wishbone pushed the ball a short distance with his nose, then swam up to it. He pushed the ball a little farther and then swam up to it again. He repeated the process a few more times, then realized he had another problem. He was exhausted.

Wow! It takes a lot of energy to swim and push a basketball at the same time. All that running didn't help, either.

Whew! . . . I don't even know if I can make it to the shore. No, I don't . . . think I can. My legs are so tired that they're trembling!

Wishbone noticed all the ducks watching him curiously from across the pond. He looked over at Joe, but the boy was too far away to see how serious the problem was. Everson was much closer, but he certainly couldn't be counted on for help.

A wave of panic swept over the dog. "Help!" Wishbone shouted. "Dog overboard! S-O-S for the D-O-G! Somebody, anybody, get me outta here!"

"Stop playing around with the ball!" Joe called out, not realizing Wishbone was in trouble. "Just get out of the pond! You're not supposed to be in there, Wishbone!"

"Don't you get it?" Wishbone yelled frantically. "I *can't* get out! For barking out loud, I'm not a seal! Help! I'm drowning!"

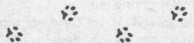

Okay, really quickly, let's hurry back to our friend Ishmael. His ship just went down, and I fear he's in danger of drowning himself!

Chapter Fifteen

The swirling whirlpool that pulled down the *Pequod* also began pulling me down. Round and round I went in a wild circle, then down and down. I was sucked roughly into the underwater darkness of the ocean. My breath was quickly giving out.

No, I told myself. *When Queequeg was very sick, he used his will to recover, and, by thunder, I can do the same!*

With every ounce of my strength, I fought my way to the surface and broke through the waves. I gulped in great breaths of air, while treading water with all four legs.

"Hallo!" I cried out at the top of my tired lungs. "Is anyone alive?"

Sadly, there was no answer. I realized my shipmates had all drowned. Every last one of them. I feared I might join them soon, despite my efforts. Already exhausted, I wouldn't be able to stay afloat much longer, and there wasn't a patch of land for more than a thousand miles.

Suddenly something burst out of the water beside me. I paddled madly away, fearing it might be Moby Dick's spout. But then I saw an oblong object shooting high into the air, soon crashing to the water. As the object floated on the waves, I realized it was Quee-queg's coffin.

I dogpaddled over. Using the very last of my strength, I lifted myself on top of it with my front paws. At Queequeg's request, I had made sure the coffin was sealed water-tight, so I knew it would float just fine. Bizarre figures and symbols were carved into the wooden lid. The markings were very similar to Queequeg's tattoos. I didn't know what they meant, but I found the idea humorous that a coffin, an object of death, was to be my life-saver.

Soon the water eased into blue tranquility. Hours rolled slowly by . . . then days. Alone I floated in the infinite ocean, Ishmael, the outcast. When night fell, I was surrounded by boundless stars and darkness.

Though scared, without food, water, or companion-ship, I somehow clung to hope. The sun and moon smiled warmly, bringing no storms. Frequently, sharks glided across my path, but they never bothered me. Was some unknown force protecting me, I wondered, or was I just fortunate?

I spent a lot of time thinking. Indeed, there wasn't much else to do. My thoughts drifted toward memories of land. I found myself homesick for such things as digging through real dirt and chasing after cats.

I thought of my brave and forever lost sailing com-panions. Their only tombstone would be the million-year-old rolling waves, but I would remember the men always. Crazed Ahab, responsible Starbuck, the man from the Isle of Man, red Tashtego, black Dagoo, others—and, of course, my purplish-yellow friend, Queequeg. I wondered if the *Pequod* had been fated for disaster, or if the ship was merely a victim of Captain Ahab's deadly obsession.

I also thought of Moby Dick. Was he a creature of evil, or merely a magnificent animal fighting for survival?

Had he perished by the sharp barb of Ahab's harpoon, or did he yet roam the ocean's depths? Could a creature so powerful ever die? Yes, Moby Dick loomed in my mind as mysterious as the universe itself.

Once more, I remembered the sermon given by the wise and white-haired chaplain, Father Mapple. He had warned that everything in the universe contained many meanings. Queequeg believed the same thing. I saw how this philosophy could apply to either a gigantic White Whale or a wheelbarrow. Or a coffin. I urged myself to keep my mind as wide and fluid as the water upon which I floated. After all, my open-mindedness had allowed me to befriend Queequeg, and, in a funny sort of way, he had saved my life.

After several days adrift, I spied sails on the distant horizon. I howled out with all my power, waving one of my front paws. Oh, how I wept for joy when I saw the white sails grow larger and larger, approaching me. Like a loving mother would do with her pup, that ship drew me into its arms. Soon it carried me back to my native land.

That ship was the *Rachel,* the very one searching the seas for the captain's missing child. Alas, I was the only orphan that wandering vessel ever found.

Ishmael's drama is done. I suppose we could spend a lot of time thinking over this whale of a novel. But instead, I think we had better get right back to my other adventure. Don't forget, I'm fighting for my life in the depths of the duck pond!

Chapter Sixteen

"Joe, help!" Wishbone yelled as he struggled to stay afloat. Thoroughly tired, the dog's body was slipping deeper beneath the duck pond's surface.

Wishbone saw Joe start to hobble toward the pond, but the boy didn't seem to understand how desperate his pal's situation was.

"Hurry!" Wishbone yelled. "Run! Now! I'd ask these ducks to help, but, frankly, I don't think they care if I live or—"

A loud sloshing came from the other side of the pond. Wishbone jerked his head around to see Richard Everson wading through the water. The high-school boy was so gigantic that the water didn't even reach up to his jacket. Wishbone realized Richard Everson, the menacing and monstrous White Whale of Wilson High, was heading straight his way!

"He's coming after me!" Wishbone cried out, trying to set his rubbery legs in motion. "Help! Help! Help!" Also alarmed, the ducks were now quacking like an off-key church choir.

"Hey, Everson, what are you doing?" Joe shouted.

Saying nothing, Everson stepped through the water with long strides. The next thing Wishbone knew, Everson grabbed him around the middle and swept him up. Then Everson carried both ball and dog to the shore, where he gently set Wishbone on the ground.

What's going on? Wishbone wondered, as he felt solid earth beneath his paws. *The Whale didn't demolish me. He saved my life! Wow! It's amazing how wet water can be. Here, let me dry off a little.*

Wishbone gave his fur a good shake, splattering water far and wide. As he did, Everson stepped out of the pond and extended the basketball to Joe.

"Here's your ball," Everson said in a quiet tone.

Joe took the ball in his hands, looking very confused. "Uh . . . thanks. I guess."

"Well," Everson said, "I shouldn't have taken it in the first place."

"Well . . ." Joe said slowly, "why did you?"

"Yeah, why did you?" Wishbone echoed before giving himself another shake.

Everson stood there a moment, his drenched jeans dripping water onto the ground. He looked at Joe and spoke, very simply. "As you seem to know, I was put on temporary suspension from the school basketball team. But I'm not sure you know the reason why. You see, Wilson has a rule stating that if any player has a failing average in any of his classes, he can't play sports until he pulls the average up. Well, I flunked my math test this week, which gave me a D-minus average in that class. So I was temporarily booted off the team."

"Oh." Joe looked thoughtfully at the ground.

Hmm, Wishbone thought. *So the big guy wasn't suspended for unsportsmanlike conduct, after all.*

"I got the news two days ago," Everson continued. "Man, was I mad. Basketball's the only thing I do really well. This morning I just needed to go walking. By myself. I came all the way to Oakdale because I didn't want to run into anyone I knew. I felt like if anyone mentioned the suspension to me, I might pop 'em one—even if they just wanted to say how sorry they were."

"Yeah, I know the feeling," Wishbone said, realizing Everson wasn't such a bad fellow. "Everyone you see starts looking like one of those cats you just want to chase up a tree."

"When your ball bounced over to me earlier in the day," Everson told Joe, "I . . . uh . . . really had no plans of stealing it. But then your friend said a few things to me and . . ."

Joe nodded, seeming to understand.

Everson let out a heavy sigh. "I never steal things. Really, I don't. But, you know, it was like I had all this anger I needed to . . . blow off somehow."

"And stealing Joe's basketball was your way of doing it," Wishbone said with a nod. "Not a very good way, but then, hey, you're only human."

"When I was shooting baskets on the playground," Everson continued, "I was already thinking about returning the ball to you, but . . ."

Joe nodded again. "But then, after we squared off on the court, I made a comment about you being suspended, and that made you angry all over again. So you ran away. Then I made an even worse crack and you threw the ball in the pond."

The hefty high-school boy knelt down next to Wishbone. "It really hit me what a jerk I'd been when I saw this little fella floundering around in the water. This is a great dog you've got here. I can tell he'd do anything for you."

Everson began petting Wishbone.

"Ah, that feels wonderful," Wishbone said, settling onto the ground. "You know, Everson, I can tell a lot about people by the way they pet me, and I think Joe and I had you figured all wrong. You're not a brute. You're a good guy after all. It just goes to show, there can be all sorts of explanations for the things we see. Uh . . . could you go a little lower, please? . . . Yeah, perfect."

Wishbone closed his eyes, enjoying the moment. He could feel the sun had brightened, and he began to hear some kids playing in the distance.

"I've acted a little dumb myself," Joe told Everson. "I got it stuck into my head that you were the world's number-one meanest basketball player. You shouldn't have taken my ball, but I probably shouldn't have jumped to conclusions, either."

Wishbone opened his eyes. "No, you shouldn't have. You might have saved me from a near-death experience. Not to mention being humiliated in front of a bunch of ducks! But don't sweat it, Joe, I made the same mistake."

"You know, that ball's a little old," Everson told Joe. "Maybe I can buy you a new one."

135

"Oh, no," Joe said, running a hand over the worn ball. "I've got others. I just like this ball because my dad gave it to me shortly before he passed away. That's why I wanted it back so badly."

Everson shook his head shamefully. "Now I feel even worse about this. I wish there was some way I could make things up to you."

Joe extended a hand to Everson. "Don't worry about it. By the way, I'm Joe Talbot."

Everson stood and gave Joe's hand a shake. "I'm Richard Everson."

"I know," Joe said. "I checked you out on the Internet. Your playing statistics are amazing."

Wishbone rose to his feet and offered a paw. "And my name, sir, is Wishbone. It comes from the canine word for 'brave and strong.' Oh, yeah, it also means 'intelligent, considerate, and incredibly handsome!'"

Everson chuckled, then gave Wishbone's paw an easy shake. "Good to meet ya. Listen, both of you, I'm really sorry about all this. Instead of going around causing trouble, I should just get my math average back up, right? Not only am I out of play until then, but I don't even get to practice with the team."

Wishbone saw how sad Everson was about that situation.

Joe scratched his neck, thinking about something. "You know," he said, "I'm always looking for someone challenging to play basketball with. I'm trying out for my school team next year, and I need all the experience I can get. I'm nowhere as good as you, but if you're really desperate for someone to practice with . . . I'm available."

Everson smiled. "I'd like that, Joe. Really. And from what I saw a little while ago, you've got a lot of promise. But maybe I can teach you a few secret tricks. Things I've picked up over the years. In fact, why don't you and I hit that court right now?"

"Your jeans might be too wet," Joe pointed out.

"The sun's out now," Everson said, looking up at the sky. "My jeans will dry off soon enough. In the meantime, I can still shoot. Hey, do you happen to have a ball on you?"

Joe laughed as he held up the ball with the "J" on it. "Oh, I guess we can just use this one!"

Everson gave Joe a sporting slap on the arm, then jogged through the park.

Joe looked at Wishbone, smiling as bright as a lit-up scoreboard. "That guy is right," he said fondly. "You really are a great dog. Come on." Joe tucked the ball under his arm and ran after Everson. His knee seemed to be perfectly fine now.

Wishbone flew after the two boys, very pleased at how grand the afternoon had turned out. *I really got all I was asking for today, and then some,* Wishbone thought with joy. *Plenty of adventure, a dose of enlightenment, a few bites of coconut candy, and a brand-new friendship with Richard Everson. And on top of that, my buddy Joe's playing is bound to get a big boost. Now that he's got the White Whale* and *the White Dog coaching him!*

By thunder, I've had a terrific time here. Like Ishmael, I feel I've traveled across the vast waters of the world, expanding my horizons in a big way. And I can tell you this—in all literature there is no better book than *Moby Dick* to inspire a person to think BIG!

About Herman Melville

Herman Melville was born in 1819 in New York City, just a few blocks from the waterfront. This was appropriate for a man torn all his life between civilization and the wild freedom of the sea.

Melville's family was originally wealthy. Later, they lost their fortune. Then the teenage Herman was forced to take a number of odd jobs. At the age of twenty, he served as cabin boy on a merchant vessel bound for England, an experience that certainly stirred his imagination.

Two years after that, Melville signed on for a lengthy whaling trip. Unhappy with the voyage, however, he escaped from the ship to a Polynesian island in the Pacific Ocean. For a month Melville lived among friendly cannibals, but when the islanders wanted to introduce Melville into their tribe, the young man fled.

He joined the crew of another whaling ship, and this time he left the vessel at the island of Tahiti. Then he joined a third whaler. Finally, after serving briefly in the U.S. Navy, this "uncommon common sailor" gave up the life of a seaman.

He hadn't gotten the sea out of his system, though. Once he was back home, Melville entertained his family and friends with his seafaring tales, and they convinced him to write them up in the form of a book. He did. In 1846 he published his first novel, *Typee,* which told of his unique experience among the cannibals. The book was a big success, and Melville felt encouraged to write several more similar novels.

In 1851 Melville published a more in-depth work, *Moby Dick*. The public, however, found the book too "weighty," and sales were poor. However, Melville continued to write stories that were challenging and complex, many of them involving the sea. Notable among these was the novella *Bill Budd, Sailor*. To help make ends meet because of low book sales, Melville was forced to take other jobs, his last being Deputy Inspector of Customs for the New York City seaport. Appropriately, his office looked out on the waterfront.

Melville died in 1891, a forgotten man, but he lives on today as one of the world's finest and most daring authors.

About *Moby Dick*

Very much like a whale, the novel *Moby Dick* is a thing of gigantic size and haunting mystery.

In a sense, *Moby Dick* is really three books rolled into a single volume. It's partly a thrilling action story, partly an in-depth study of whales and whaling, and partly a philosophical exploration of man and the universe.

In this last direction, *Moby Dick* ventured further than any novel yet written at the time. While keeping the story's sense of high adventure, Melville also explored important themes and ideas through his use of symbolism. This means that certain realistic elements in the story can also be viewed with a larger meaning. For example: The *Pequod,* with its multi-national crew, can be seen as the Earth. The sea, huge and always shifting, can be seen as the human mind. The white whale, both threatening and splendid, can be seen as the whole universe. Of course, every reader is free to interpret these symbols in any way he or she chooses.

Because *Moby Dick* presented such an unusual kind of writing, it was looked down upon at the time of its publication. Most of the reading public wished Melville had written another exciting but simple sea yarn, or tale, like several of his previous works. The book got bad reviews by critics, and it sold poorly.

In the 1920s, many years after Melville's death, *Moby Dick* was rediscovered—in a big way! Scholars praised it, many people read it, and the book came to be thought of as one of the world's great masterpieces of literature. With its well-imagined characters, rich language, and deep meanings, *Moby Dick* was compared to the epic poems of Homer, the plays of Shakespeare, and even the Bible. A well-known author of the time, D. H. Lawrence, spoke for many when he wrote of *Moby Dick,* "It moves awe in the soul."

Moby Dick has been performed both as a play and as a movie, analyzed in numerous critical studies, and taught in classrooms. Most of all, however, it is there to delight readers of all ages with its great power.

About Alexander Steele

Alexander Steele is a writer of books, plays, and screen-plays for both juveniles and adults—and sometimes for dogs. *Moby Dog* is his first book for The Adventures of Wishbone series. He has already written *Tale of the Missing Mascot* for the WISHBONE Mysteries series.

Mystery and history are favorite subjects of Alexander's. He has written seven detective novels for young readers, and he is at work on an adult novel that deals with the origin of detectives in both fiction and reality. Among Alexander's plays is the award-winning *One Glorious Afternoon,* which is based on Shakespeare and his fellow players at London's Globe Theatre.

Alexander first attempted to read *Moby Dick* when he was around Joe Talbot's age, but he fell overboard somewhere in the middle. Shortly after college, he finally made it through to the last page, and it was a voyage well worth the effort. He read the book again while preparing this adaptation, and he became completely fascinated by Melville's masterpiece. He hopes *Moby Dog* will inspire some of its readers to one day make their way through the five-hundred-page original, *Moby Dick.* Not only is it an unforgettable story, but people will be really impressed!

Alexander lives in New York City, where there are no whales, but there are plenty of people chasing after taxis.